W9-AUP-581

The Locked Crowns

"He was the stalworthest man at nede
That may riden on ani stede."

The Lay of Havelok the Dane

Books by Marion Garthwaite

COARSE GOLD GULCH

MARIO

MYSTERY OF SKULL CAP ISLAND

HOLDUP ON BOOTJACK HILL

THE LOCKED CROWNS

The Locked Crowns

by

MARION GARTHWAITE

Illustrations by

HERMAN B. VESTAL

DOUBLEDAY & COMPANY, INC.
GARDEN CITY, NEW YORK

Library of Congress Catalog Card Number 63-12880

Printed in the United States of America

to E.L.G.

Foreword

The name of Havelok is not on any list of English or Danish kings. Havelok the Dane is a legendary figure like Arthur and Robin Hood. An English version of the story appeared in epic verse about 1280 A.D., in the reign of Edward the First. There are other English versions and also a French variant called *Le Lai d'Haveloc*. These differ in details, but the essential story is the same. The several versions make it fairly certain that the story was told and sung for many years, centuries probably, before it was written down.

The Rev. Walter W. Skeat says in the preface to his re-editing from 'the unique manuscript of the Lay of Havelok the Dane' in the Bodleian Library at Oxford, "On the whole let us place Havelok in the sixth century at *some* period of his life."

These early folk of the north are part of our American history through the voyages of Leif the Lucky. They were a sturdy, enduring race, not always brutal and barbaric. Their restlessness drove them as far south as the Mediterranean, as far west as the North American continent, centuries before Columbus. Both pagan and Christian, they feared death and were unafraid to die. They were lawmakers, and set and held to the penalties for the breach of law. Their jewels and woodcarvings were of fine workmanship, rich in design. Their women's weaving was firm and beautifully patterned.

They had an innate and abiding love for poetry and a well-told tale, and the music that went with these.

They were skilled boat-builders of graceful, seaworthy craft that skimmed the wave-ways like seabirds.

They wielded a strong sword, a swift stone, and kept their battle axes keen.

Contents

The Locked Crowns

i

Athelwold

The story of Havelok the Dane is a tale of treachery and the wickedness of men who wanted two rich kingdoms for themselves, and so betrayed the royal children in their care.

In the beginning there was a princess. She was a very small princess, too young to walk or talk. Her father was King Athelwold, overlord of Britain, but the tale tells us nothing of the queen who was her mother.

The princess was named Goldborough. She was dearer to King Athelwold than all of his kingdom, or even his life. Because of her his last few days were full of dread.

Before his death Athelwold lay sore-stricken, in a high wall bed at one end of the king's hall at Winchester. He raised himself on one elbow to let his steward stuff some blue and violet pillows behind his head. He sank back into them with a groan, his face gray with the effort it cost.

"Edwy," he said to the steward, "send Solvi here to me."

The steward smoothed the soft fur coverlet of the high bed. "And the leech, Sire?"

"No, Edwy." The King raised his hand and let it drop. "I have no more need of leeches."

Before he made his way out of the hall, the steward laid a chunk of wood on top of the glowing coals in the hearth pit. He pushed open the heavy iron-studded door. He stopped by a group of men standing in the garth between the hall built of well-chinked logs and the kitchen built of wattles and mud.

"Is he better, Edwy?" asked one of the men hopefully.

"He is worse," the steward answered heavily. "He can neither eat nor sleep. Have you seen Solvi, Harald?"

"He is polishing the King's war gear. He is certain that Athelwold will want it when he is well again."

Edwy turned away. "He will want it whether he lives or dies. It will be needed for the funeral pyre."

"It will be a sorry time for England, if he dies now," said Harald, "with only a baby girl as heir." He stared down at the dagger in his hand. "Who will rule us until she can?"

No one answered. Each of them turned the thought over and over in his mind. Who would have the power of life and death over all of them in the long years ahead?

The men were dressed in leather and fur against the sharp fall weather. They stood about beyond the men's door of the hall under the roof of the open porch that had been newly built to hold off the winter snows. One man was honing a dagger, another was braiding some leather thongs. Each man worked at something, but they were waiting. Waiting and talking. Talking about the dying King. Thinking about the baby Princess.

Harald struck his dagger deep in a log and pulled it free

again. "I cannot bear to have him gone," he said. "He has been a good king, just and fair in all his dealings."

"My father is a dealer in hides," said the man braiding the leather thongs. "He says that all the merchants bless this king's name, because he has cleared the woods and towns of the robbers and outlaws that plagued them. He has hung the worst of these thieves from the gallows tree, and all the land has been at peace."

And so they talked of him. Of the fierce loyalty this dying king had gained from earl and thane and serf and thrall, because he was righteous and strong, unafraid, and a good Christian king.

"He has hewn a path straight through the trees," said Harald. "He has imprisoned knights and even lords, all of high or low degree who broke his laws."

The steward returned. With him he had Solvi, a short, dark, and stocky man dressed in a leather tunic, belted at his waist. At some time Solvi's nose had been broken, but his black eyes were merry and there was good humor in the three-cornered shape of his lips. Around his neck was a thrall-ring of iron. They passed the men gathered under the eaves of the porch, and went in to the King's bed.

Smoke curled up lazily from the hearth fires, but the long hall was full of shadows. The early light beneath the lowering clouds scarcely lightened the oiled skins that covered the high windows.

"Here is Solvi, Sire," said the steward.

The King opened his eyes. "My thanks to you." He made a slight move with one hand, and Edwy left them.

Solvi stood beside the bed, his sorry eyes on the gaunt figure of Athelwold.

The King looked back at the thrall, his face serene and unafraid. "You have been a good thrall, Solvi," said Athelwold, "and I know you for an honest man. Now I have one more task to lay upon you. It is to guard the Princess with your life. When she is grown and safely married to some strong man who can help her rule England, you will have earned your freedom. At that time you can strike the thrall-ring from your neck. If you choose, you can go back to Wales, where you were captured."

"I would rather stay with you for life, Sire," answered Solvi.

"So you shall," said the King. "So you shall. It will be but a short stay. From the chest that I will leave with Hild, you are to each have ten links of Irish gold. This will bring you land and oxen, and pay you for your years of service."

"Sire, I need no pay for this."

"You may have need of the gold to guard your lady," said the King. Solvi said no more.

The King reached under his pillow and fumbled about until he brought out a roll of parchment. "What I have said is set down here. This will grant your freedom and Hild's. Show it to the Princess when she is old enough to understand. To no one else, unless there is a question of your freedom when your lady is safely wed." The King closed his eyes.

Solvi took the parchment and tucked it inside his tunic. "I will guard the Princess with my life, Sire," he promised.

"Good." The King stirred and groaned. "Fetch Hild to me, and ask her to bring the little maid."

A few minutes later a serving woman in a kirtle of

wadmal cloth came to the King's bed. Her long hair was in neat braids, her sandals slapped on the stone floor. She was a plain woman with a wide mouth and steady hazel eyes.

In her arms was a small girl in a long dress of soft blue stuff, embroidered at neck and sleeves and hem with silver thread. The child's fair hair was the silver-gilt of ripened wheat, and lay in shining, silky curls about her face. Her cheeks were flushed with sleep. Her sea-blue eyes were full of wonder as she stared about her at the painted shields and weapons on the walls, at the hound dog that rose, stretching and yawning, his long tail thumping against the wall bed.

Suddenly the baby caught sight of Athelwold. "Da!" she shouted, and held her chubby arms out to the King. Her eyes were alight and all eight teeth were showing as she laughed.

A wave of color stained the cheeks of the King. He started to raise his arms and then dropped them. "I have no strength. Does 'Da!' mean me, Hild, do you think? Is this her first word?"

Hild laughed. "I'm sure it is, Sire. She is shy with the rest."

"Does she walk yet, this little one?"

"Almost. Look, Sire." Hild sat down on a painted chest. She stood the little girl on the floor. Hild moved her knees away and the baby stood alone, rocking on her bare feet, curling her toes against the cold of the stone. Then the child plunged forward and buried her face in Hild's lap, gurgling with glee.

The King chuckled. "It has been good to see her. Bring her again and yet again. Now send her away."

Hild took the baby to the women's door and handed her to someone there.

"Stay with her, Hild, when I am gone." The King's voice was worried. "When she is safely married, then you are free to go. The chest you have been sitting on belongs to her. It is her dower. I am putting it in your care. Open it."

Hild opened the lid of the chest. On the top of dry packed moss lay a small circlet of gold with a single blue stone glistening in the front of it. Hild picked it up carefully.

"To crown her Queen of England," said Athelwold, "when the time is come."

Hild lifted the dried moss. Underneath packed in more of the crisp, gray stuff were pins and buckles, the glitter of rings and arm bands. There were links of Irish gold, and a necklace of thick-set, honey-colored amber.

"You will keep the chest with you, Hild, as though it were your own. Let no one know you have it. Stuff the top with linen or toys, whatever you have. It is an old chest and looks to be of little worth." Athelwold leaned back into the pillows, his eyes closed.

Hild packed the moss back with care, and laid the small gold crown on top.

"When the Princess is married, she is to give you ten links of gold for your own marriage portion." The King sighed and winced as pain stabbed through him. "I have put it in writing. Solvi has it. It tells of your freedom and his. Guard her, Hild. I feel I can trust her to you and Solvi."

"Oh, Sire!" Hild's mouth was twisted with grief. "I promise."

The King turned his head away. "Send Solvi for all the earls and lords from Roxborough to Dover. Tell him to bid them make haste on an urgent matter. There is not much time." He drew a ring from his finger. The red stone was deeply graven and the carved crest had been inlaid with gold. "Tell Solvi to carry this ring with him. It will tell the earls and barons more clearly than his word that I have need of them."

Solvi saddled a horse and rode off into the misty morning. The ring lay heavy in a doeskin bag hung around his neck. The rose hips in the hedges glowed like rubies. The trees were a riot of red and gold. The air was crisp beneath a sky so blue it made Solvi's heart ache for the King, who would not live to see another season all gold and blue like this.

Solvi stopped at Chester where the old Earl heard his news with real grief. When the Earl had sent runners out with the summons to the mead-halls east and west of him, he drew on his ox-hide byrnie all overlaid with rings of iron. He gathered his men about him to ride to Winchester.

"This is a sad day for me," he told Solvi. "And for England as well. A man can travel from one end of the land to the other these days, with no fear of loss. Alas! Who will rule this country now, until the little maid is grown?"

Solvi had no answer to this. He rode on through that night and the next, snatching a few hours of sleep beneath a haycock before he borrowed a fresh horse and left his own behind. He traveled along a paved road built by the

Romans that led south through England. Wherever he carried the word and showed the ring, the King's men girt on their swords and made ready to ride.

Even the common folk were sorry when they heard his news. "King Athelwold has pitied the fatherless," said one thrall who met Solvi at the gate of his master's hall. "Even the bread of his own table was not too good to feed the hungry at his door."

Solvi could see where there might be hungry men at this hall. The moat was choked with reeds. The fence of stakes that stood above the earthen wall was broken and rotted. Inside the hall the rushes were rank and muddy and moldy. Beyond the hall the fields lay in uneven strips with weeds along the ditches.

At the sight of the ring this knight too made ready to journey north. "We will have to choose some strong earl as ruler," he said, "until the Princess is grown."

It was late at night when Solvi came to the hall of Earl Godrich of Cornwall

He was turned away by the man at the gate. "Ring or no ring," growled the guard, "my life would not be worth a bitten penny if I woke the Earl at this hour."

"I have a message for Earl Godrich from the King," said Solvi.

"The King's business will have to wait. The gates were locked at sunset."

"The King dies and would summon his earls for counsel."

"Then like enough Godrich will make himself the king. He bows to no man. He can learn of this tomorrow." The man turned away from the high gate beyond the bridge of logs over the moat.

Solvi found food for his worn-out horse on the common field below the town. He found a bed for himself beneath a tree.

The next morning he could tell well enough that this stronghold was no slovenly boar's nest like the last one. The river water ran clear and swift in the moat. The earthen walls were steep and well tended, with the stake fence high and sharp and close set. Guarding the gates were log houses for armed men. Above the doors of the hall were the widest-spreading antlers that Solvi had ever seen.

"You will have to wait your turn, thrall," growled the steward when Solvi presented himself at the hall door. Solvi showed him the ring. After that the steward put him in a place close to the high seat.

When Earl Godrich entered with his knights in full armor to attend him, the waiting people dropped to their knees. Solvi did likewise but with little grace. Athelwold had not asked this of his people. There had been courtesy and friendliness, but little knee-bending, at the English court.

Solvi was the third person to go up to the high seat. He kneeled as he had seen the others do, and kissed the hand that the Earl put out to him. He handed the King's ring to the Earl.

Earl Godrich turned it over and over in one hand while the other stroked the silky black moustache that drooped about his full lips. His hands were white as suet and loaded with rings, but there was breadth and power in his heavy shoulders.

"Why does Athelwold send me his token-ring?" he asked.

"Because the King lies ill, even unto death. He has sent word to all of his earls and barons and knights of high degree to come as soon as may be to Winchester for a Parliament."

"This is news!" Earl Godrich leaned forward. The rich silk of his tunic changed from violet to green as he moved in the firelight. "Athelwold's child? How old is she?"

Suddenly Solvi felt afraid for the little Princess, but he could see no way out of it. "She is scarcely a year yet, Sire."

"And Athelwold thinks to turn England over to a puling babe?" Earl Godrich laughed. His black eyes, almond-shaped in a narrow face, glittered with malice. He clapped his hands. "Bring me armor and saddle horses for ten armed knights. Pack clothes for a lengthy stay, and what food we need for the road. I may stay longer than Athelwold has bargained on. I will want my war gear."

He was in great good humor as he waved the rest of the waiting people away. "You will ride with us, thrall," he said to Solvi.

"My horse is lame. He needs a day's rest, Sire." Solvi thought the Earl would offer him a fresh horse as others had done.

Earl Godrich shrugged. "As you like. It would be a safer ride with me."

"The King's ring—" began Solvi, eying the ring on Earl Godrich's thumb, where the red stone glimmered.

Earl Godrich turned his back and walked away, carrying the King's ring with him.

Solvi did not dare to ask for it again.

In a few days' time the earls and knights were gathered about Athelwold's bed, sore-weeping when they saw him brought so low.

"Hold your peace!" he said to them sternly. "I have need of your counsel, not your tears."

Edwy raised the King so that he could sit back against the pillows. "Your weeping cannot help me now, since my candle is burned down to its last hour. But I pray you, bring me peace of mind in my going. Tell me in whose charge should I put England and the little maid who will be your lady?"

Then there was muttering and whispering and a great shaking of heads over this name and that. When all had agreed upon a name, the old Earl of Chester stepped forth as the spokesman of the lords.

"Earl Godrich of Cornwall, Sire, is strong and greatly feared. He would guard the maiden until she comes of age to rule."

The King agreed to this. He ordered an embroidered cloth to be brought, of fine linen, fair and close-woven. Upon this was placed the Mass-book.

Earl Godrich kneeled there with his hand on the Book, his eyes, black and close-set, upon the sick man in the high bed. He repeated after the King a solemn oath. "I swear to be a true and faithful guardian to the maiden Goldborough," he said, so that all in that room could hear the words, "and to govern this realm until she is of age to marry. At that time I promise I will give her to the fairest and strongest man in all England, and deliver the kingdom into her hand."

When this had been sworn the King closed his eyes in great weariness of spirit. He roused himself once more. "To you, Godrich of Cornwall, I give in trust this land of England. I place in your care my child, the Princess Goldborough, until she is of age to rule in her own right."

The King began his prayers as his loyal knights fell to their knees about him. When he had said, "Unto Thy hands, O Lord–" his voice faltered–ceased–and they knew their beloved King was dead.

The bells tolled and the people wept as the earth was piled in a high how over the funeral pyre of Athelwold, with his horses and hounds about him.

When the days of mourning were done, Earl Godrich took all of England under his rule.

He put strong knights who had sworn fealty to him in the larger halls. He made all manner of people put their hands in his as a sign of their willingness to serve him. He placed justices in the courts who would do as he said, and appointed sheriffs and magistrates to rid the woods and byways of any who stood against him. When he had all England under his strong rule, he could do as he chose. All in the land were afraid of him. He ruled them with a heavy hand and waxed rich and strong.

Through these years Goldborough, the daughter of Athelwold, grew in beauty and in wisdom, until she was the fairest lady in all the land, skilled in housewifely arts, gracious, and kind.

When Earl Godrich heard men say that the Princess was fair and chaste, and that she was the rightful ruler of

England, he was angered. Why should this weak maid be queen? he thought to himself. Why should I give up this rich land to a foolish girl and make her my lady? I have been too easy-going, too gentle with this strong-willed Princess. I have a son. England shall be mine, and my son's after me.

So Earl Godrich let go of the oath he had sworn. In secret he took Goldborough away from the castle at Winchester, where she had been born. He walled her in a high tower of rocks, close by the sea town of Dover. He fed and clothed her in unseemly fashion for a maid who was royal-born. He let no one visit her, or even know where she was being held a prisoner.

Goldborough had no way of knowing what she had done to bring this bitter treatment upon her. She never saw the Earl of Cornwall. The two servants, Solvi and Hild, who waited on her, knew no more than she why she was so treated. But in their hearts there was great fear for their mistress.

As for Goldborough, the only comfort she had was the friendship of the two who served her.

It was a sad time for the daughter of Athelwold. She wept as she walked the weary round of the high tower, her eyes on the seething sea. Her days were filled with prayer and stitchery. Her beads and her tapestries both were bathed in tears, until her heart was like to break.

ii

Havelok

Two boys squirmed their way through the close-matted whin bushes until they reached an open space. All about them the hillside was warm and spicy beneath the westering sun. Below them there was a sharp glint of water where the river had spread over the marshy meadows that led down to the sea, a sea that stretched eastward from the coast of Denmark.

The taller of the two boys wore an over-large tunic of heavy homespun cloth that came halfway to his knees. The long sleeves were rucked up to his elbows. His eyes were a surprising blue in a dark face, beneath close-cropped black hair. He had the high cheekbones and straight nose of a well-bred Dane.

"Did you s-see which way the bee went, Havelok?" asked the second boy, trying to get his breath. All the smaller boy wore was a pair of doeskin trousers that he had to keep hitching up over his narrow hips, and two rings of twisted wire in his ears.

The taller boy grunted in disgust. "No. I was watching,

too. By the time we got through that tangle she was gone. She was loaded with pollen, and she flew so low, so slowly, I thought we'd keep up."

The small boy squatted down in the shade of a high bush. "Whew! It's hot! Let's s-sit here and wait. If we see another one we'll know which way to climb."

Havelok stretched out on the sparse straw of the summer grass and wiggled himself comfortable. "Can you sew well enough to mend this tunic, Hugh Raven? I've torn the shoulder of it." He twisted his shoulder off the ground to view the three-cornered tear. He eyed a long scratch on his forearm and sucked off the beads of blood.

"I can s-sew," answered Hugh Raven. His speech was slow, because if he hurried, sometimes the words would not come at all. "But coaxing a needle from Gunnild is s-something else. S-she's s-stingy with needles." He turned a dusty, anxious face toward the other boy. "Which s-shoulder?"

Havelok grinned. "Stop fretting. The cross is on the other side. Even with such a big tear the mark won't show."

Hugh Raven sighed. "Lucky for us, then. If anyone s-sees the king-mark, none of us will ever get away from Denmark alive."

Havelok sat up and hugged his knees. "Your brother, William Wendut, said there was another man this morning asking questions about the boat. Did you see him?"

"No. But I think that is why we were s-sent off to find a bee tree. My father does not want s-strangers asking questions about the new boat or the new boy we have.

Above all he does not want you questioned by one of Jarl Godard's men."

Havelok waved this aside. "Godard will never send anyone here who knows me. He would never dare to let any of his jarls know how he killed my sisters and gave me over bound and gagged to be drowned. It would give the one who knew about this treachery too much power over Godard for him to take that risk."

Hugh Raven rolled over on the dry grass and squinted at the roots of Havelok's dark hair. "Not a gleam," he muttered.

"Better not be," growled Havelok, "after Gunnild's been dousing my head every day or so with that oak gall mess."

"Just the s-same," said Hugh Raven, "if Jarl Godard guesses that you were not in that s-sack my father s-sank in the s-sea, the rabbits will be in the s-stew. It would be the end of the house of Grim."

Havelok pushed his sleeve up and looked at the pale skin of his upper arm. "I'll be glad when we get to Norway and I can take off this stuffy tunic. After these months in prison my arms are as lily-white as any girl's."

Havelok's eyes filled with sudden tears. He turned his head away angrily, lest Hugh Raven see it.

"You watch that way," said Hugh Raven, "and I'll watch this. If you s-see a bee flying, heavy-laden, raise your hand. We'll follow her."

Hugh Raven knew that Havelok's tears were for his two sisters, Helfled and Swanborough, murdered by Jarl Godard.

Havelok turned back to face Hugh Raven. His jaw was

set and his eyes were almost black with anger. "You mark my words. For what Godard has done he will some day pay. I will come back to this land he has stolen from me, since I am the rightful king. Then it will be Havelok against Godard. Either the new white God or the power of Odin must choose between us. Win or lose I will have done what I could to avenge my sisters." His eyes were bright with unshed tears. "The day will come," he said between clenched teeth.

Hugh Raven shook his head. "It's not the way of the new teaching," he said.

The younger boy's eyes were as hard as agates. "It's my way. Godard was my father's man. He agreed before a hundred knights at the *thingstead* to raise me and my sisters as was right and fitting for us. Instead he threw us in a filthy hole, a dark dungeon of a room, with almost nothing to eat and without even a fire to warm us."

"If you come with us," said Hugh Raven, "you will have to believe in the white Christ. We are Christian folk. All but my mother. S-she tries to believe as my father does, but s-she will not cross the upper bridge of logs where the creek comes down. S-she thinks there is a troll there."

"Godard is the troll. He is all the powers of evil rolled into one ugly troll. He has taken my heritage. He killed my two sisters. He tried to take my life, and will yet. As soon as my father Birkabeyn was dead, Godard took over all of Denmark. Men who were freemen and thanes, under my father, with lands and oxen and decent homes, are Godard's thralls now. They live in mud huts and fish for what pennies they can get for food and clothes for their families."

"There was more to eat than fish in the days of Birkabeyn," agreed Hugh Raven. "Then my father was a freeman. Now he is Jarl Godard's thrall. The Jarl hasn't made him wear the thrall-ring, but he took our lands and hall, and our oxen as well."

Havelok watched a small field mouse pull down a stalk of grass and nibble off the seeds. "It was a bitter day when Godard came to see us in that grimy hole." He dug his bare toes in the dirt and the little mouse scurried off into the furze bushes. "Helfled and Swanborough had wept all night from hunger and cold. I tried to be brave enough for all of us, but my knees shook with the cold of the stones, and my fear of this wicked man. I tried to greet him fairly, as the son of Birkabeyn should have done, but my heart was sick at the mad look in his eyes."

A bee flew across the clearing, the pollen baskets on her legs full to bursting. Hugh Raven marked her flight, but he did not raise his hand. A soft little wind stirred the grasses, and a lark soared into the sky with a ripple of song.

It was better for Havelok to talk the bitterness out of his heart, thought Hugh Raven. Far better for him to talk to Hugh Raven and the sun and the sky and a soaring lark, than to some stranger who might cajole him into saying enough to hang them all.

Hugh Raven looked over at the younger boy, who was a head taller than he was. In many ways Havelok seemed older than Hugh Raven, who was nearly ten. Havelok could speak the Latin tongue as well as his own. He knew many things about hunting and horses and weapons. At other times he seemed young and spoiled, and given to lording it over the sons of Grim. William Wendut and Hugh Raven laughed at him and forgot it. Robert the Red, the eldest of Grim's sons, was angered and grew sulky.

"He is our king," Grim had pointed out to them.

"Not yet," Robert the Red had answered shortly. "When he is, I will follow him wherever he leads. Now he is a boy with no kingdom and a grave danger to all of us. Just look at his lordly ways. Do you think anyone will believe our tale of a dim-witted cousin come to live with us, when they see this boy ordering us all around? They will know well enough he is no serf's son. We will all hang for taking in this lordling."

Hugh Raven was remembering all of this as he watched Havelok sitting back on his heels, chewing on a grass stem.

"I told Godard that we had naught to still our hunger," Havelok went on. "I belittled myself for the sake of my sisters. 'Lord!' I cried. 'Is there no corn for men to grind into bread to give us? We are very near our deaths.'"

Hugh Raven watched another bee cross the open space, but he did not stir.

"That fiend cared nothing for our misery. Before my eyes he laughed as he cut my sisters' throats. He tossed them in two pitiful heaps against the stone wall. He caught me by my long hair and forced my head back. I saw the gleam of the knife at my throat. I knelt down on the cold stones and begged of him, 'Lord, have pity.' I cried out to him." Havelok choked on the words.

"Well, but what else could you have done?" asked Hugh Raven in his slow voice.

"I don't know." Havelok squirmed at the bitter memory. "I don't know. I dream it over and over. In my dream I am brave and strong, and save my sisters. I promised Godard my homage and all of Denmark. 'Let me live!' I cried. 'I will swear on the Book never to bear weapons against you. I will leave Denmark. I will never return.' All this I promised, if he would let me live."

"You have just s-said you would come back s-some day," Hugh Raven pointed out.

"I will come back. I will return and reclaim my own. He did not mean to let me live, that Judas. It is true he did not kill me then. My tunic had fallen from my shoulder. I saw his eyes on the king-mark, and on the light that comes at times from my mouth. I think he was afraid. He drew back his knife—truly it was a miracle. He flung me on the stone floor and left me there to weep over my two dead sisters."

"How long were you there?"

"I have no way to tell. But Godard was not through with me. He did not have the courage to do this thing himself. But he knew he would never feel safe on the throne of Denmark until the rightful heir to it was dead."

"He s-sent for my father," said Hugh Raven. "A thane of Jarl Godard's, a black-browed man on a s-streaming wet black horse met us one night as we ran our boat up on the s-shore. He told my father that Jarl Godard wanted to s-see him. My father s-said he would come when the mackerel run was over. The man just laughed at him. 'Be there by tomorrow noon, Grim Fisherman,' he s-said, 'or lose your boat.' S-so my father went there, though Leve, my mother, wept at this."

"Then what did Godard do?" demanded Havelok.

"I listened that night from my bed in the wall. My father s-said Jarl Godard called him a thrall. 'You know well enough, Grim Fisherman, that a thrall must do his master's bidding. I will make you free again, and rich beyond your dearest dreams, if you will take a child I have here, wrap him in a s-sack, and when the moon is bright, cast him into the s-sea.' He s-said, too, 'If there be a s-sin in this I will take it for my own.'"

Havelok gave a snort of anger. "He has so much sin on his soul now, he is bowed down with the weight of it."

"My father told my mother that Jarl Godard took him into an inner room where there was a boy with fair hair, lying against the wall bound hand and foot."

"Me," said Havelok. "And a black curse on his wicked soul for it."

"My father was afraid not to do Jarl Godard's bidding. He took the boy. Under the Jarl's eye he wrapped him in a heavy cloth. He gagged him with foul rags the Jarl gave him, until he could not s-speak, and only barely breathe. He put him in a huge black s-sack and brought him home to our house s-slung across his back."

"I was more dead than alive, trussed like a pig for sale, bumping and swinging and swaying until I was dizzy."

"I heard him bring you in. I heard him tell my mother what he had done, and all that Jarl Godard had s-said to him."

Havelok laughed. "Dame Leve was so startled she jumped up and knocked me over. My head cracked against that big stone by the fireplace. I thought it was the end of me. Right then I wished I had never been born a king's son."

"My father and mother did not know what to do." Hugh Raven watched another bee wing its way across the small clearing. "At midnight they were afraid to wait longer. My father put on his heavy s-sea clothes. My mother was s-surprised that s-she could s-see him do this in the night. There was no candle lit. There was a light that s-seemed to be coming from the s-sack by the hearth. How do you make that light, Havelok?"

"I don't. It comes and goes. Often when I have been in danger I have wakened to find it shining around me."

"My mother s-said it was like a s-sunbeam from your mouth. It made a light as bright as s-seven wax candles burning in the room. My mother was afraid. 'What light is this s-shining in our house, when we have lit no candle? Come quickly, Grim, and tell me what it is.'"

"They took me from the sack and unbound me," said Havelok. "When they turned back my shirt they found the king-mark."

"It was bright and fair on your s-shoulder. Even from behind my bed curtains I could s-see it. My father was s-sick with fear and grief. He touched the cross on your s-shoulder. 'God knows that this is the King of Denmark,' I heard him s-say. He fell on his knees s-saying that he and Leve, my mother, were your thralls. They s-said that they would keep you and guard and feed you until you were old enough to ride out with helmet and s-spear to claim your kingdom."

"I will, too."

"My father s-swore that Jarl Godard s-should never know. He s-said he would take his freedom from no one but you."

"It is good to know that there is one loyal Dane," said Havelok, moodily.

"There are s-seven. Grim, my father, and Leve, my mother. There are my two brothers, William Wendut and Robert the Red, and my two s-sisters, Gunnild and Levive. And—of course—me."

Havelok reached over to pat Hugh Raven's knee. He was grinning. "That's a good start. Even when I have all Denmark for my own, I will never forget the first seven who took me in and risked their lives to feed me and get me safe away."

"You are not s-safe away," Hugh Raven pointed out. "There are too many s-strangers asking questions, and the boat is far from finished. It must be big enough to carry all of us and all our goods. Robert the Red is the best builder of boats on the coast of Denmark, but even he cannot bend wood and s-step a mast in a few days' time. Every day we s-stay here, the risk is greater. My father must keep on fishing to give us dried fish to eat on the journey. My mother and s-sisters must go about their work as though no journey were planned at all. My mother is baking the hard s-ship's bread from all the flour s-she can get."

"Do your sisters know we sail for Norway?"

"Yes."

"They are older than we are. They will not tell."

"None of us will tell. From that first night we have s-sworn loyalty to you as our king. Robert the Red s-says it is you who will give us away and hang the lot of us."

Havelok sat up, flushed with anger. "I will not!" he shouted. "Who says I will tell anyone I am King of Denmark and risk the necks of all of us?"

"We all do. Look at you now. S-shouting it out for anyone to hear. You have not learned to hide your pride. You cannot be a s-stupid cousin one minute and a kingling ordering us all around the next."

Havelok thought about this as he watched a hawk circling in the sky. The hawk stooped on the lark they had heard singing, missed in his headlong plunge, and flew up for a second try. The lark dove for safety in the thick brush as the hawk came whistling down.

Godard is the hawk, thought Havelok. He can stoop to pluck us off one by one, if I give us away.

"If we come through this venture," said Hugh Raven, "we will follow you to your death, or ours."

Havelok was shy of this outburst, and willing to change the subject. "How I ate that night! Dame Leve must have been sorry she offered to feed me."

"I was the s-sorry one. My mouth was fairly watering there behind my curtains. I watched her bring you the best of all we had, bread and pasties and cheese cake. I can hear her now. 'Eat then, Lord, that we may prove our loyalty to you.' I was s-starved!"

Havelok laughed. "It had been many a long day since I had seen decent food, bread and cheese and honey. . . ."

"Honey!" cried Hugh Raven. "'Lok, there's been a long line of bees headed for home. The sun is nearly down. If we want honey for dough cakes, we must follow them before the s-sun is s-set."

The two boys sprang to their feet. They started up the hill following the bee line, with Havelok in the lead. Hugh Raven was carrying the linen sack they hoped to fill with honeycomb, hitching up his trousers as he climbed.

"Grim made a fair bed for me, of clean warm skins," panted Havelok, as he pushed ahead. "He undressed me and laid me in it as tenderly as a mother might have done. He said, 'Sleep then, my son, sleep fast and sound. Naught shall harm thee, so have no fear.'"

"That's easy enough to say," said Hugh Raven gloomily, as he put one foot above the other on the tough and tangled stems of the heather and gorse. "It will be easier to do when we are all s-safe away from Denmark and Jarl Godard." He caught hold of a bush to pull himself up. "I hope we find this bee tree. I'm s-starved!"

iii

Jarl Godard

That night with Havelok asleep in the bed beside him, Hugh Raven lay awake tossing and turning. The fiery burning of his bee stings would not let him sleep. His face was swollen and feverish, his arms and chest and back a mass of angry welts.

Gunnild had gone over him carefully to pluck out all of the stingers, and had washed the stings with a soothing lotion.

Havelok had only a few stings and these were nearly gone by the time the two boys were home again with their precious sack of honeycomb, dripping with golden sweetness.

Hugh Raven had asked Havelok, "Why do they come at me like a furious army with drawn s-spears, while they leave you with only a s-sting or two?"

Havelok laughed. "Perhaps it is because Brother Wilfrith of the Priory taught me how to soothe them, if I would rob their hoard. Or," he added with a grin, "it might be because Hugh Raven is a sweeter bite for bees than Havelok, the bitter."

To keep his thoughts from his torment, Hugh Raven was going over in his mind that first night when Havelok had been brought in on Grim's shoulder in the black sack.

After Havelok was asleep, Grim had filled the sack with chunks of wood from the hearth place, and three heavy stones from the garth. When he saw that Hugh Raven was awake Grim told him gruffly to get dressed, that he had need of him.

Hugh Raven had put on his warmest clothes and followed his father out into the night where wisps of sea-fog veiled the moon.

Grim carried the heavy sack on his back, bent over with the weight of it. They went down to his boat where Grim set the sack on the river bank until he and Hugh Raven had pushed the boat down into the water. When she floated freely on the sucking wavelets of the river mouth, Grim lifted the heavy sack over the stern onto the floor boards. He climbed into the boat to take the oars, while Hugh Raven pushed the boat away from the slick mud of the shore and clambered in.

"Watch," whispered Grim, "while I row. If you see aught of anyone on either side, tap your foot against the sack, twice if the north bank, three times for the south."

Grim rowed slowly away from the shore. Hugh Raven sat in the stern watching the high banks of the river mouth. Was there a shadow on the south bank? The moon came from behind a cloud and the figure of a lone horseman showed clearly against the southern sky. Hugh Raven kicked at the sack.

Grim did not vary his stroke. He turned his head slowly and the boat swung enough to the left so he could see the figure on the high bank. "Aye," he muttered, "I had thought it would be like that."

Shreds of fog shut out the moon's light until Hugh Raven could no longer see the watcher on the bank.

Grim rowed slowly out beyond the river's mouth into the open sea. When the fog lifted and the moon was shining again, he shipped his oars and stood up in the rocking boat. He picked up the sack, heaving it over the gunwale on the south side of the boat and into the water.

In his mind Hugh Raven could still hear the froglike plop and the sullen splash, as he and his father watched the heavy sack sink at once beneath the heaving swells. Hugh Raven shuddered as he thought of the boy asleep by the fire, a boy who had been tied hand and foot inside that black sack.

Grim rowed back to the shore of the river. He and Hugh Raven pulled the boat up to the sea grass, out of reach of the incoming tide. They watched the dark rider turn his horse and ride off beyond the edge of the cliff.

Grim carried the oars over his shoulder as he and Hugh Raven went home to the crowded house. In a nest of skins by the hearth the strange boy slept, his fair hair in a tangled halo around his face, a strange glow shining between his half-open lips. Beyond the sleeping boy were the carved posts of the high seat, brought from the big house after Birkabeyn's death, when Grim had been made Godard's thrall.

Grim stood looking down at the shining head of the

boy. Hugh Raven stood beside him and Dame Leve hovered behind them.

"Who is he?" asked Hugh Raven.

"It is Havelok, the rightful King of Denmark. But we have drowned him, don't forget, in that black sack we threw overboard into the sea."

"And now what shall we do?" whispered Dame Leve, wringing her work-worn hands. "What do we do now, Grim—now that he is drowned but we have an extra boy on our hands? What do we do? Tell me that."

"We sleep on it," answered Grim.

The next day as soon as their night's fast was broken, Grim had ordered Havelok's fair hair cut short and dyed.

Havelok did not want his hair cut. "My hair has always been long like this," he said haughtily. "Only thralls wear their hair close-cropped."

"Aye," said Grim shortly. "Wear it long then, and let Jarl Godard know, the first time you set foot outside this house, that we have a fair-haired long-hair newly come to the house of Grim. Or stay within this house day in and day out, while we prepare a boat to carry us all to safety. Or will you roam abroad with your long fair hair blowing in the wind and hang the lot of us?"

So Havelok had let Gunnild cut his hair and dye what was left with an evil-looking dye she had brewed of nut hulls and oak galls and roots gathered in the woods. She brushed this dark dye over his fair eyelashes and eyebrows with a stick she had chewed and dipped in the mixture. She washed his face and hands and arms with the same dark stuff.

"Only until the sun has browned your prison paleness," she told him.

Havelok became Hugh Raven's charge. "Stick to him like moss to an oak," Grim commanded his son. "Your brothers will be working on the new boat all day and most of the night. I must keep fishing to bring us in food enough for now—this boy eats as much as two. We need still more fish to dry for our journey. Gunnild and Levive must finish the new sail. Your mother will get our war gear in order. And all the while we must go about our affairs as though we had naught on our minds but a fishing trip."

"They can see that the new boat is bigger than we need for fishing," said Hugh Raven.

"I shall give it out that my two brothers have joined me in the building of this boat. It is for all three of us to share."

The day after Havelok had come Grim dressed himself with care for his visit to Jarl Godard's court. The whole family was gathered about the fire indoors in the early morning. Havelok sat with them shoveling down a thick porridge covered with clotted cream.

Dame Leve begged Grim not to go. "Why do you not let well enough alone, Grim? The boy is drowned. You tell me that Godard's man saw you do this. Stay here and leave Jarl Godard be."

Grim went on combing his gray hair and the grizzled moustache that sprouted from his upper lip and flowed down to his chest. "Jarl Godard promised me my freedom, and riches besides. He would know that something was strangely amiss if a thrall failed to come back to claim them."

"What do we call this child?" demanded Robert the Red, frowning at Havelok. "We'd better call him something other than Havelok, the King's name."

Grim pulled on a small cap of skins and a fur tunic. It was hot for fur, but it was the best he had to go before the Jarl. "We will call him Bjorn, the Bear Cub. For any who ask he has come to us from kinfolk to the East. He will live with us, since his father was killed on a reindeer hunt and his mother died of the milk sickness. We must say that he is the same age as Hugh Raven though we know he is younger. They will think him over-large for his age and thick of wit. Get him away, or let him be dumb if anyone asks too many questions. From now until we sail Hugh Raven is to stay with him like a dried burr to a cow's tail."

"We will keep them both busy," said Gunnild, her brown face merry. "They can churn the butter for us. It will free us to work on the sail."

"Churning is woman's work," said Havelok. "Let the maids churn the butter."

"We are the maids," said Levive tartly, "since my father became a thrall."

"We can use some help in this house," agreed Gunnild cheerfully.

"If anyone comes," said Grim taking up a heavy staff, "get the boys into the woods. Or put them in Hugh Raven's bed behind the curtains, with Havelok beneath the blankets and next to the wall."

"I will choke to death!" cried Havelok, furious.

"Perhaps you like it better bound and gagged in a sack," suggested Grim. "Burn his clothes," he told Dame Leve. "Keep the pin he wears on his shoulder and the ring from his finger. Bury them beneath the hearthstone. Dress him in a tunic of William Wendut's, since Hugh Raven's clothes are too small for him."

William Wendut put down the knife with which he was carving the handle of a wooden spoon. He ran his long fingers through his straw-colored hair. "That will leave me one tunic for the journey," he said ruefully, "unless Gunnild will weave me cloth for another."

"We shall have luck with us if Levive and I finish the new sail," answered Gunnild. "We have both looms set as wide as they will stretch with linen threads."

"I will go into the woods and live!" cried Havelok in fury, "since I am such a burden to all of you."

Grim turned on him, his gnarled hand on the bar of the door. "And have us all flayed alive as soon as you are caught poaching the Jarl's pheasants? You will stay here well-hidden, king-born, until I think it is wise to let you out, if you would get away from Denmark with your life."

Dame Leve hovered over Havelok, her hands fluttering. "He is our king," she was whispering over and over. "We must not talk to him like this. He is our king."

"Cease your clack, Dame," said Grim. "He is also a noose around our necks. I did not save him from the sea to let him hang us and himself as well, on the nearest gallows tree."

Then Havelok was ashamed. He said no more but let Dame Leve take his clothes and cast them in the fire. He put on a well-worn tunic of William Wendut's that hid him well enough under heavy folds of wadmal cloth, and covered the king-mark on his shoulder.

As soon as it was daybreak Grim set out on the long walk to see Godard. He did not look like a thrall except for his close-cropped hair, but more like a prosperous merchant journeying through the oak and beech woods on his way to the nearest town for a meeting or for trade.

He made his way to Godard's hall, a long two-storied log house. This was surrounded by a high mound of earth topped with a palisade of sharp-pointed logs. There was a moat of half-stagnant water from a nearby stream.

Grim took his place at one end of the hall with other men seeking the Jarl's favor. He could see Jarl Godard sitting in the high seat, with knights and jarls and barons to right and left of him.

Fires burned in pits in the earthen floor. The smoke curled upward to be lost in the murky rafters where ancient painted patterns in blue and red, with here and there a gleam of gold, showed through the blue haze. Shields and weapons hung on the walls. Before the seat where Godard sat there were skins of bear and deer spread out on the rushes.

Godard himself was richly dressed in a blue silk shirt embroidered at neck and wrists with gold. A blue cape edged with fur covered his shoulders. This was pinned close on one side with a fibula of blue agate.

Grim did not see the Jarl glance his way, but in a short while a man in the clothes of a house carl touched him on the elbow. "The Jarl will see you now," he said in a low voice, "if you follow me."

So Godard is still Jarl, thought Grim. He thinks the

heir to Denmark's throne is dead, but he has not yet dared to make himself the king.

The servant took him down a long hall where the open windows were hung with closely woven tapestries and the rushes were fresh-strewn and smelled sweet and clean.

At the end of the hall they entered a small room. The wait was neither long nor short. The Jarl entered alone and closed the door behind him. He stood with his back to the heavy door, scowling at Grim.

"Well?" he asked in a grating voice.

Grim could see that the Jarl's shoes were cut high, gilded and stitched in red. He had earrings of red stones dangling from his ears.

Grim stood fast, his hand on his staff, his cap on his head. "I threw the sack into the sea weighted with stones," he said. "I have come for my freedom and the riches you promised me."

Jarl Godard's eyes seemed to sink into his skull and a purple pulse throbbed on the shiny side of his bald head above his ear. His fingers plucked convulsively at the sapphire silk of his sleeve. "So!" His voice was cold and harsh. "You think to be a jarl now, is that it?"

"I would be a freeman," answered Grim sturdily, "as was my father and my father's father."

Jarl Godard's laugh was like the neigh of a frightened horse. "Get thee gone, churl, back to the dirt from which you came. A thrall you have been," he snarled, "and always will be." He leaned closer to Grim, his lips drawn back over his teeth. "One word from you, Grim, fisherman, and I will send you to the gallows. Crow meat is the cheapest meat at the market."

Grim took his weary way home in the day's heat. "The Jarl could do no less," he told Dame Leve. "He would not dare to pay a good price for last night's work, lest I guess who it was I threw into the sea."

"What must we do, then?" she asked. But she knew the answer as well as he.

"We must get away as swiftly as may be. There is no refuge in Denmark for any of us now. If Godard knows that Havelok lives he will kill all of us, the boy first of all. It is best for us to flee the land if we would live."

Dame Leve turned away with a little whimper.

Grim looked after her. "It is hard for men to pull up roots," he told the two younger boys, "when they have lived and loved in the land of their fathers. It is heart-breaking for women."

While his two sons worked feverishly on the new boat, Grim set about selling his goods. Each day after he returned from his fishing Grim trudged about the countryside, selling his woolly sheep, his horned cow, his sow and her piglets, and the bearded goat. Even the geese of his farmyard and the speckled hens and cock were sold.

Grim shrugged when his neighbors asked him why he was selling all his goods. "I have angered the Jarl," he told them. "He has levied taxes against my land that I cannot pay from my boat and crops alone."

His neighbors pitied him in his trouble, and paid him good money for his beasts and fowls. They paid him in copper coins from many lands and a few silver pieces. All of these Grim put away in small stout sacks against his sailing.

When Havelok's hair was cut and dark he was allowed

out in the sun and wind, with Hugh Raven close at hand. If anyone outside the family stopped at Grim's stead, Gunnild sent the two boys into the woods for berries or watercress or wood, for anything she could think of to get Havelok out of sight.

Havelok himself took pleasure in acting like a dull clod. He would stand behind Hugh Raven, sniggering and pursing his lips, squinting his eyes against the sun, scratching his bare brown toes in the dust.

Hugh Raven was slow of speech as well. The two of them seemed too stupid to bother with.

Havelok would have liked to work with Robert the Red and William Wendut on the new boat. But he was inept with tools. The older boys felt they had no time to teach Havelok what he needed to know to be of use. They would lose patience with the two younger boys and send them off with curt words.

Hugh Raven had always had a multitude of duties from cutting and hauling the wood for the fires to cleaning the fish. Havelok had spent his days under Birkabeyn with studies in Latin and kingship, with learning to ride and to hunt with weapons, with dogs, and with falcons. Until his father's death and his own imprisonment, his days had been full to the brim with the work of learning to be a leader of his people.

Now both boys had time on their hands and orders to keep out of sight. The shady forest was at hand to hide in. Once the wood was stacked and the fish gutted and strung on the lines in a clearing behind the house, they were free to fare off to the woods.

Everyone was too busy to keep track of them. Havelok

was only too glad to keep out of sight, if Hugh Raven could go with him. Gunnild would give them a bit of cooked meat wrapped in a dough cake as thin as a leaf of kale, and send them off to the woods. Both boys found this to their liking.

They roamed the edge of the woods from the road down to the sea sand and spent hours lying in the sun watching all the busy woods life about them.

This was how matters stood in the house of Grim the day that Havelok and Hugh Raven found the Finn man in the place of the rune stones.

iv

Pakkanen

Havelok and Hugh Raven came upon the rune stones by chance late one afternoon. It was after they had climbed up the stream bed above the old mill. The roof of the mill had fallen in but the water still splashed over the wooden wheel, dripping down on the black and slimy paddles. There was a smell of blackberries ripening in the sun. All about their feet there was a yellow-flowered creeper, and a rank weed dusty with feathered seeds.

"There is a new mill now," said Hugh Raven. "Jarl Godard built it between here and Vejle. We Grims fish mostly, but we also raise some corn for bread. We must pay the Jarl a full s-share of any grain we grind."

"Why not grind it at home, then?" asked Havelok. "Couldn't you make a hand quern of hollowed rock?"

"And have your nose s-slit or your ears cropped? The Jarl knows to the last grain how much a plowman harvests. It is the Jarl's right to demand what he chooses of the crop. From now on my father knows that Godard would demand more and more from him, until it would not pay to make a crop. Then we would have to live on fish or else s-starve."

Beside a mound above the mill the boys came upon the rune stones. There was an open level space beyond the mound, all girt about with a thicket of thorn. A giant oak stood at the head of this open place. Close to the oak there were five of the carved stones. Each one of them, almost twice as high as Havelok, was rounded at the top. They were covered with strange figures of birds and beasts, all interlaced with twined bands. Two of them leaned one against the other. The other three had fallen to earth, and the flowery grass was knee-high about them.

Havelok was leaning over the fallen stones. "Here's something! These stones mark a king's grave, I think." He was tracing with one finger the old twisted symbols carved in the stone.

"Can you read it?" asked Hugh Raven.

"Of course not, you ninny. I can read a little Latin and that's all. This is older than Latin, I think. See, here is the eight-legged horse of Odin and here is the Fenris-wolf. The men who carved these stones believed in the Norse gods."

"I think we s-should not be here," said Hugh Raven fearfully. "There is no cross anywhere on that s-stone. It is a pagan thing."

Havelok laughed. "Whoever carved these stones is long gone. To Heaven—or else to Valhalla—"

"Or to Hel!" Hugh Raven's eyes flicked into the shadows beneath the huge oak tree ahead of them. "They s-say that s-sometimes a man's s-spirit comes back to a place like this—Ai-ee-ee!"

From behind one of the fallen stones a figure rose. He stood upright in one fluid motion. He was a short man, lean as a wolf. His leathery face was burnt almost black, and heavy-lidded eyes were set deep on either side of a hooked beak of a nose. He had a wily face, with humor in the folds of his eyelids and the sideways twist of his lips. His eyes were a bright blaze of ice-blue in his dark face and his teeth were white and even. When he pulled off his small leather cap his hair was black and curly.

Hugh Raven turned to run but Havelok stood forth. "Who are you, stranger? What are you doing here beside the rune stones?"

The man hitched up his ragged leather breeches, tied about his waist and each ankle with frayed rope. He reached down and gathered up a large square of woolen stuff and wrapped it about his shoulders. "I am a Finn," he said in thick Danish. "I am called Pakkanen. I slept here this night on a bed of leaves until you wakened me." He stooped down again to pick up a flat bundle wrapped in brown sailcloth from behind the stone. "This is my harp, my *kantele,*" he said with a certain dignity. "I am a singer, a scop."

Havelok was delighted. "I have not heard a singer since my father died. Singers came to us from as far off as—"

"Come, cousin!" Hugh Raven plucked urgently at Havelok's sleeve. He turned to the Finn. "He is s-slow of wit," he explained. "Half the time he does not know what he s-says."

The Finn smiled a slow wide smile. "He does not sound so slow," he said softly. He unwound the sailcloth and

struck the strings of the small harp with his long fingernails. The notes fell like crystal drops on the summer air.

Havelok reached out to touch the harp, his eyes alight with pleasure.

"It is made of reindeer bone," explained Pakkanen, "bolted together with silver pegs. The keys are of silver, but the inlay in the bone, the pattern of leaves and flowers, is of mother-of-pearl."

"Sing, Pakkanen," commanded Havelok sitting down on a fallen rune stone.

"We must go home," argued Hugh Raven. "We have come too far afield."

"Oh, be still!" said Havelok. "This man is a singer."

As though that explained perfectly why they should stay and talk with this stranger. With Havelok acting like a king's son and no dim-witted cousin, Hugh Raven was at his own wit's end.

"Tell us first what news you bring, Singer," said Havelok, pushing Hugh Raven's clutching fingers from his sleeve.

"I come from Jarl Godard's hall," said the Finn, watching the two boys warily.

Havelok's face lost its glow. "Did you sing for the Jarl?" he asked, trying to keep his voice careless.

"No. My clothes were too mean for Jarl Godard's court. They turned me out." The Finn shrugged. "I was glad to go. I had seen enough to think the Jarl would not have liked my Kalevala songs. He did not even spare me a crust of bread against my hunger."

Havelok was indignant. "My father would never have turned a singer from our hall."

"No." The Finn ran his fingers up and down the gleaming strings of the little harp. "As for news, I heard in the market place that Jarl Godard plans to crown himself the King of Denmark next Easter when men come to pay scot and settle their tithes with the church."

"Were they pleased to hear this," asked Havelok in a small voice, "there in the market?"

"No," answered Pakkanen. "Only the men of the court have any love for Jarl Godard, because he has put them where they are. The rest will wait as long as they must for Birkabeyn's son."

Havelok lowered his eyes to hide the fierce gleam of joy in them. Hugh Raven turned away sick at heart. The hares were in the stew-pot now, he was thinking.

"Perhaps Jarl Godard will see to it that this boy does not grow up to be a king," Havelok suggested.

The Finn nodded. "A good chance of that. If this boy could get away from Denmark—but it must be soon—he could bide his time and fight for his crown when he is old enough to wield a sword and shield."

Havelok grinned up at the bland face above him. "You know too much, Finn," he said with a short laugh.

"I know this," answered Pakkanen. "Each day the sun crosses the sky and the young King stays, the time of the Jarl's knowing comes closer. Look! You think I know too much. I will tell you something. Last night I killed a hare and roasted it for my supper. In my bag behind that stone is a fresh-killed partridge that just happened to walk into a few sticks and string I had at hand. Now, king's son, we are even. I can hang you—and you can hang me."

Havelok laughed joyously. "Ho! Hugh Raven here, Grim's son, is green with fear for me."

"And so he should be," answered Pakkanen. "You give yourself away each time you blink an eye or shrug a shoulder. Let me come home with you and talk to Grim. I too am afraid for you."

As they scrambled down the slope below the rune stones Havelok asked, "Do you always sing Kalevala songs, Pakkanen?"

"Not always. I like them best, since they are the songs of my people. But each to his own. A singer looks to his listeners when he sings. In England I sing of Beowulf and the two dragons. In Ireland I tell the stories of Cuchulain who could run wind-fast and catch his own thrown spear."

"How did you know I am the King's son?"

"My father brought me to Denmark ten—no, twelve years ago. We sang in Birkabeyn's court for Christmas and three months beyond. Except for your hair you are as like him as two eyases hatched in the same nest."

"My hair is dyed to keep Godard from knowing I was not drowned by Grim."

"I thought as much. But it is not enough. Every move you make brings your father to mind. Grim did not know Birkabeyn. He would not know how plain it is for anyone to see."

"He is reckless too," grumbled Hugh Raven. "I am s-set to guard him from s-strangers, but he gives himself away before I can s-stop him."

The Finn laughed. "A trained falcon does not become a barnyard duck for wanting it."

Levive met them on the old stream bank above Grim's house where the woods began. She was breathless. "There is a stranger—" She stopped in fear and confusion when she saw Pakkanen.

"It's all right, Levive," said Havelok. "He is the Finn, Pakkanen, a singer who knew my father. This is Levive, Grimsdatter."

Levive made the best of it. "Since you know," she told Pakkanen, "then I can tell you that a man has come named Horda. He is a Norse man and now of Godard's hall. He is ugly and brutal with a pocked face and hairy hands. He has been asking about the boat, about our selling our stock. He says he saw two people leave the house this morning, to go into the woods. He will wait, he says, until they return. The way he looks at us—the way he asks his questions . . . He knows about Havelok—I'm sure he knows." She began to cry.

Havelok put his face against her arm and rubbed it along the coarse cloth, trying to comfort her. He felt he could not bear to see Levive cry.

"Perhaps we could fool this Godard's man," said Pakkanen briskly. "He saw two people go, and two people will come home. Give me your tunic, king's son, and here is my cloak."

Havelok peeled off his tunic and wrapped the long square of tattered cloth about him. He slung an end of it over his shoulder and went strutting about, posing and posturing like a singer.

Pakkanen turned to Levive. "Go back, lady. Send a call to us when you are nearly home. Hugh Raven will answer. The king's son can bed down here in the woods until dark. When this Horda is gone, we will put a rush light at the stable end of the house. If there is no light, and he gets too sleepy to watch longer, a night in the woods will but toughen him."

Levive hurried down the steep path with Hugh Raven and the Finn close behind her.

Havelok made himself a pile of fresh leaves. He sat down upon it, drawing the cloak about him. He was wide awake, listening for Levive's call. When it came it was so clear and seemed so close at hand he was almost startled into answering it. He heard Hugh Raven's shout, and settled back into the ferns.

He fingered the Finn's bag and felt the body of the bird the Finn had trapped. He was tempted, in his hunger, to light a fire and cook it. Common sense warned him that a single spark from his flint might be seen from below.

He watched the sun set and the stars prick out. All about him were the tiny quick green sparks of fireflies winking in the dusk. Below him he could see the light of the driftwood fire Grim had built outside his house. With strangers there, and one of them a singer, they would sit up for a time in the long, shadowless twilight to listen to the Finn.

It seemed unbearably lonely to look down upon, out of the high wild rune-stone place. Everyone knew that fires flickered over these graves at night, and sometimes led a man deep into the forest, until he fell into a bog hole or a deep pit where the ox-knee people lived.

Havelok started as a little whispering sound stirred in the thorn bushes. Sadness ran through him like a hot cup of broth. All the memories of his happy, busy boyhood came crowding in upon him. His father's pleasure in the singers who came with news and entertainment, the long tables loaded with food, his dog, Bran, his sisters playing in the inner court. He could even remember in a far away time his mother's white hands on a harp. He had a sudden quick bright memory of fires burning on the hills on Midsummer's Eve.

There was another rustling in the bushes. His heart began to pound. An owl hooted like an idiot's laugh. There came a shriek of mortal agony, and death pounced on something deeper in the woods.

Havelok sprang to his feet. His eyes were straining to see into the dim reaches of the trees. His knees were shaking. Was that something moving? Did he hear a breathing close at hand? What was that? He kept his head turning and twisting to meet each new danger, each rustle in the undergrowth, as the shadow-shapes crept closer in the summer night.

Why stay here in these dark woods in the glooming,

haunted by who knew what? Why not go closer to the fire below, and so hear the music and the talk? It might be wise, he tried to reason, to see this Godard's man, to know him if he met him once again.

No one heard or saw the boy who came down through the trees behind the house. Havelok sat down in the shadow of the plow shed out of the light of the fire and the gleaming crescent moon that hung like a small sickle blade in the evening sky.

Two men were seated on a log, face to face, their hands on each other's shoulders, swaying back and forth as they chanted the story of the Sampo from the Kalevala. One of the singers was the Finn. The other was a man Havelok had never seen before. Strange, he thought, how the first sound of music brought neighbors you did not know. He thought at first it might be Horda. But later when Robert the Red moved to put a log of wood on the fire, Havelok saw Godard's man sitting on the ground beside Grim.

He was much bigger than either of the singers. He looked like the crafty, slit-eyed man Godard would send to do his bidding. Havelok did not know this man by sight. So perhaps Horda would not know Havelok. But had Horda ever known Birkabeyn? That was a thought to chew on. Havelok drew back behind the wooden plow. He turned his face from the fire and pulled the Finn's cloak closer about his head.

Even in the firelight Havelok could see the pockmarks on Horda's face. An unkempt beard that had been bleached to a rusty yellow with lime and had the texture of a hempen rope that had come unraveled, straggled down to his chestbone. His belly bulged over his nail-studded leather belt, and his helmet had the farthest spreading horns Havelok had ever seen.

The men's voices rose and fell on the night air, as first one and then the other picked up the verses.

> "Far away I see an island,
> Dimly looming in the distance,"

sang the deep voice of the man Havelok did not know. When he fell silent, the story of the Sampo went on in Pakkanen's clear tenor that rose and fell and held in some way the quality of a harp string.

> "Then the aged Väinämöinen
> Spoke aloud the words which follow:
> 'Row thou smith; row, Ilmarinen;
> Row, O lively Lemminkainen;
> Row ye also all ye people,
> That the boat be hurried forward,
> And the vessel onward driven.'"

Was there a warning to Grim in these words? Havelok searched the shifty eyes of Horda, the calm eyes of Grim. He could not tell.

The fight for the Sampo was a struggle for power, a tale of treachery. Havelok too had met treachery. His head whirled as he thought of it. Could Grim get his family and Havelok away from Denmark before disaster met them all head-on?

Havelok blamed himself for the lazy days he and Hugh Raven had spent in the woods. And yet—what could he do but keep out of sight, lest the twist of a shoulder remind men of the King they had respected and loved? Or bring home to Godard the evil he had done and the threat that this clumsy kin of the Grims might be to his peace of mind.

As the tale ended for the night with the Sampo sunk beneath the waves, Havelok crept into the stable. He waited until Levive came to set down a stone lamp filled with fish oil and knew that Horda was gone.

Havelok put out the light. He felt his way down to the house end of the building and climbed into the wall bed beside Hugh Raven. He was bone-weary, hungry, and heartsick.

From Levive's tears he knew he had brought danger and trouble to these kind people who had taken him in. He was afraid for them and for himself. He wished he could climb up into Dame Leve's lap and let her comfort him. He wished he could weep out his fears and his heartbreak.

"You are too big to cry," he told himself sternly. "You who are a king's son." He didn't feel so very big, and being a king's son had been an ugly, dreadful business, since his father's death.

There was a heavy foreboding weighing on his spirit. Would he always give himself away as he had to the Finn? Was he always to feel hunted in this land of his father's? Had Godard sent this Horda to spy on him and learn the secret of the new boy who had come to live with the Grims? Levive was sure Horda knew about Havelok. Would he tell Godard? Havelok shivered in spite of the heavy sleeping fleece he had pulled about him.

He was a long time getting off to sleep. When he did his dreams were full of strange and dreadful things. He cried out in the night and Dame Leve came to him, holding his cold hands tight in her warm ones.

"There! There!" she crooned softly, and sang him a lullaby.

> "Mary hath had a Babe in a manger,
> Sing lully, lully, soft and sweet."

He did not know when she was gone again.

v

Horda, Godard's Man

While they broke their fast in the morning, they talked of Horda. The Finn sat at the heavy hand-hewn table eating his way steadily through a plateful of dough cakes and honey, washed down with ale. Havelok sat on the floor by the hearth fire gnawing on a crisp well-peppered pheasant leg, his mouth smarting from the spice and dripping with the golden fat.

"How near done is the new boat?" asked Pakkanen. "How soon could it be finished?"

"It is seaworthy now," answered Grim. "It needs the mast stepped, and we have only one thwart braced. Besides this, William Wendut would carve a cross to hang on the mast to bless our journey."

"The mast can be stepped in a day," said the Finn. "How long will it take to make the thwarts and carve a cross?"

"A week," said William Wendut, "though the cross could take a year and still not be worthy."

Pakkanen pushed his wooden plate back. He smacked his fist on the table. "I don't think you have it."

"Have what?" asked Robert the Red sharply.

"A week."

"Why not?" asked William Wendut. "Horda was satisfied when you and Hugh Raven came in from the woods. He went off with no further questions."

Pakkanen set his lips and shook his head stubbornly. "I still think you must get away at once. There is too much talk in Vejle, and along the road to Jelling. The talk is about Godard and the kingship. And of Birkabeyn's son. Where is he? they ask. And the two little princesses, where are they? I tell you there is a muttering among the Dane folk. Jarl Godard is afraid. And when a coward finds himself afraid—" he shrugged. "As the saying goes, 'Measureless is the ill will and boding of a coward.' "

"I think the Jarl is sure that Havelok is dead," said Grim.

"I think the doubt-worm is gnawing in Godard's crafty mind," said Pakkanen. "He would not send a man like Horda here, to watch from the bushes, if he felt sure that Birkabeyn's son was dead. Why watch an empty nest? Even if he were sure, he must be sleepless by night to remember that he made Grim gag the boy and put him in the sack." He leaned forward, his heavy-lidded eyes half shut. "Soon it will be known to more than you and Godard that the king's son is gone. That—and an extra boy in the house of the man who carried him away—" he flung his hands out in a hopeless gesture. "I think you are moonmad, Grim Fisherman, to wait even for a day."

"I have told you, Grim," said Robert the Red, "how

they have watched us from the trees. There has been another besides Horda, sniffing around, as soon as the prow of the boat showed over the weeds. He asked us why we let our youngest boys run so freely in the woods. Had we no work for these idle hands? And why were we selling all of our stock?

Grim sat pulling at one end of his long moustache. At last he raised his hand. "Enough. We will sail at dawn with tomorrow's tide. This will give us a day to set the mast, and get the sail hung. We can make the thwarts as we go. The cross will have to wait until we reach a haven."

"I'll carve that, too, as we go," said William Wendut. "If the knife slips now and then in a rough sea, the Christus will forgive it. He too was a woodworker."

"One more thing," said the Finn. "No—two! First I think that now the king's son must stay hidden until you are well set on the swan's way. And second—" he hesitated for a long moment. "I would ask passage of you, Grim, on my own account, to Norway." He waited for an answer. When Grim said nothing, Pakkanen added, "I have naught but my loyalty to offer, and a fair knowledge of ships and the sea."

There was a long pause. Pakkanen sat quietly, his thin brown hands between his knees. The only sounds in the room were the little punches Gunnild was making in the tightly woven linen as she stitched the heavy sail, and the soft sound of wood ash falling in the hearth.

No one else moved or spoke. It was like a painting on a church wall, a scene from the life of a saint, caught and held in pigments of mauve and fawn-color, brown and the sooty black of the fire irons.

Finally Grim spoke. "The new boat is built for eight people and their food and goods. There are eight to sail in it. Where would you sleep, Finn?"

Pakkanen shrugged. "I can stand watch at night and catch my sleep when I can. I have sailed as far as Greece in a Viking ship. I have helped fight off Franks and pirates in those waters. I am quick with ax and spear, not so good with sword or bow."

"Why do you want to go to Norway?" asked Grim.

Pakkanen's eyelids drooped over his ice-blue eyes as he hunched his shoulders. "Why does any singer leave a warm hearth for a distant land? I have never seen Norway. They say it is fiercely beautiful. That's beckoning enough for a rootless man."

Havelok's hands were clenched. He wanted Pakkanen to go with them. He trusted the Finn, and he yearned for the solace of the scop's poems and songs. But he felt that he was lucky enough to be getting away himself. He did not know enough about the dangers of a voyage in an open boat built for eight. Would one more be too heavy in a boat like that? Havelok did not know about boats and the sea, so he closed his lips and sat silent.

"I have my family to get safe away from Denmark," said Grim slowly. "And Birkabeyn's son. I will think about this."

"That is fair enough," said Pakkanen.

"Could Hugh Raven and Bjorn bring in enough ripe berries for a last dish?" asked Gunnild, coming in with an armload of clothes to be washed. "They are ripe in the pasture, and so good. Who knows where we will find ripe raspberries in Norway?"

Pakkanen put out a protesting hand. "This time Godard might not send a man to watch. He might send ten men to find this boy and kill him, no matter who he is."

"Then too," added Grim, "the Jarl knows that Hugh Raven was with me when we took the sack out to throw it in the sea. Now that the Jarl is suspicious of this house, it is wiser for Hugh Raven to stay home as well."

"I can pick raspberries," offered Pakkanen. He took up one of Gunnild's rush baskets and slipped out into the sunny morning.

A short while later there was a heavy pounding on the door. With swift motion Havelok dove through the curtains of Hugh Raven's bed and disappeared beneath the sleeping fleece at the foot of it.

Levive stepped quickly to the bed and pulled the down pillows out onto the floor. She stooped inside to straighten the feather bed, filling most of the space between the curtains.

Grim opened the door a small crack. "Who is it?" he demanded. "Who pounds at this hour in the morning fit to bring the house down?"

"Jarl Godard's man," answered a rough voice. "Open up!"

Grim stepped aside. The man named Horda pushed through the doorway.

His small eyes darted around the room. His broken teeth showed in an insolent grin that said as plainly as words that he knew they dared not shut him out. His eyes rested longest on Gunnild sitting before the big tan sailcloth, her golden head bent over her basket of thread.

"What word do you bring, Jarl's man?" asked Grim.

"It has come to the ears of the Jarl that you are boatbuilding, thrall." Horda glanced at the sail hanging from the rollers of the two looms.

"My two brothers and I have been building a new boat," agreed Grim. "My small boat does not bring in enough fish to feed my family."

"Did you have permission from the Jarl to build this boat?"

"I did not ask. This is the first time I have heard that fisherfolk must ask to build a boat."

"It was the Jarl's trees you cut."

"True. And I had his permission to cut them two years ago. The wood was cured for a season and I have been shaping it for a season. We will pay the Jarl with the half of every catch."

"The Jarl says he has need of a boat. He sends word that you must sail your new boat to Vejle by tomorrow noon. He will pay you a little something for the labor, if he thinks the boat is worth it." He reached down with dirty fingers to feel the quality of the fawn-colored sail linen stretching downward from the rollers to the heavy warp stones. "This is good sailcloth," he said, grinning into Gunnild's startled face. "The Jarl will be pleased."

There were spots of bright color on Grim's cheekbones. "My boat is not yet finished," he said evenly. "It needs thwarts and braces and the mast stepped."

Horda yawned and scratched his arms. "I know all that."

"Will the Jarl give me a few more days to finish these things?"

"No. Jarl Godard said tomorrow. You can finish it for

him when you bring it to Vejle." Horda tramped out, not bothering to shut the carved door behind him.

Pakkanen had seen Horda ride up to the house. He had watched him tie his horse to the ring outside the door, and pound on the carved panels with the handle of the dagger he drew from his belt. The Finn put down the basket he had brought with him and turned back to the house. He came along the fence of woven willow, built to keep the goat and cow from Dame Leve's herb beds. He watched Horda lead his horse out through the gate.

Horda stood eying the slender figure of the singer with open contempt. "What is your business here, Finn?" he demanded.

Pakkanen shrugged. "One place is as good as another to a hungry man. I stop where ever my songs will buy me food."

Horda hoisted himself into his saddle. "It is a rich thrall who can feed a singer." He turned his horse and then stopped. "I was not fooled, Finn, when you came home with Grim's boy. I have watched in the woods. What I saw there was not a man and a boy. Nor was it two boys from a fisherman's hut."

"What did you see, Norse man?"

"I saw what will line my pouch with gold very shortly. And I warn you to keep your nose out of this business, if you know what is good for you."

Pakkanen laughed. This angered Horda. He leaned down and spat in the Finn's upturned face. Then he spurred his horse and rode upstream at a heavy, jolting trot.

When Pakkanen walked into the house he was wiping the spittle from his smooth-shaven face. His blue eyes were mere slits in a gray face, his lips tight.

Grim had turned to his stricken family. "We sail at midnight, against the night tide," he said heavily.

"And Pakkanen?" came the muffled voice of Havelok from beneath the sheepskin.

"The Finn goes with us, if he is still of a mind for it."

Pakkanen nodded.

Grim took a pair of oars from beside the door. "Until dark we will work as though we had nothing in mind but a sail to Vejle tomorrow. Here in this house Hugh Raven and Havelok will get food and clothing and weapons in three piles. I will look them over later."

"And I?" asked Pakkanen.

"Help the boys, Finn. You know what the boat can take. I shall need your help later with the mast and the rollers. It will take all of us to get the boat into the water."

"Can we cut the sail from the loom?" asked Gunnild. Her eyes were shining and her cheeks flushed.

"Yes," answered Grim. His dark eyes lit with laughter when she reached up and hugged him.

"It's so exciting to cut it away, Father, after all these weeks of hard work. It is Levive's and my very first piece of sailcloth."

"It is good sailcloth," said Grim. "It will carry us far. It will be the wings of the Raven boat and keep us flying over the wave-road."

"Let me have your knife, then, Father."

"Take to the stream only such clothes as will be dry by

nightfall," Grim told Levive. "Leve–" he turned to his wife and touched her pale cheek where tears were flowing in silent misery "–the hardest task of all is yours, wife. You will dry your tears and sit in the doorway, carding wool."

vi

The Flight

It was a harrowing day both inside and out. In the house Dame Leve was continually leaving her post in the doorway to bring them some treasured bit of stitchery, or a little carving William Wendut had made for her, or some pot or crock she could not bear to leave behind.

She dug up the jeweled pin and ring from under the hearthstone and pressed them into Havelok's hand.

"What shall I do with them?" he asked Pakkanen.

Pakkanen looked at the jewels and whistled. "Hide them, king's son," he growled. "Do not carry them in sight, if you value your life."

Gunnild settled that question by putting them in one of the little leather bags hanging from her belt.

Grim and his two older sons worked feverishly on the new boat. It was a small boat but built for ocean-going, a sea-rider, high-prowed and high-sterned, with William Wendut's carving on the gunwale boards. She was single-masted so that two men alone could handle her, even in a high sea.

William Wendut had forged a strong strip of iron. This was bent and bolted on the curved breast of the fierce bird that made the figurehead of the boat. Because of this iron Pakkanen called the boat *The Ice-Breaker*, but Grim had named it *The Raven of the Winds*, because his people were long since come from the raven folk.

They dared not get it completely ready in daylight, being afraid that Godard would send someone else to sail it away. They had hidden the oars in the bushes at the river's mouth. Round logs were cut and the boat eased over these down to the river's edge. Water-borne, the *Raven* rolled with the swells like a seagull, her tall mast raking the green evening sky, the water chuckling beneath her keel.

William Wendut fastened a small cross of twisted wire knee-high on the mast, and sprinkled sea water on the raven's head that bent down to meet the deep-curved keel.

Dame Leve carried with her a sprig of mistletoe. The Finn wore his amulet of twisted gold tinged with green. Havelok and Hugh Raven had their bits of iron in leather sacks about their necks to protect them from witches and trolls. Havelok also had a smooth green stone he fondly hoped was a toadstone, dropped from the head of some luckless wood toad, to guard him against poison.

After their evening meal the family sat out by the fire of silver-veined driftwood, burning blue and green. Hugh Raven and Havelok listened from inside the house, lest there be a watcher beyond the fire. Pakkanen unlocked his song-hoard for them, singing them songs from his homeland. The woods were dark beyond the fire. Some of the songs were peasant-gay. Most of them were heartbreakingly sad.

Grim had looked over the piles of gear in the house. He had left the food and most of the heavy clothing. But almost all of Dame Leve's treasures, even her woven coverlets and goose-down pillows had been put aside. Her tears at the fire were not for the sad songs of Finland. They were for a spoon, hand-carved by a small boy for his mother, or the first stitches a little maid had pricked into a linen square.

The stowing away in the boat was swiftly done, in less than an hour's time. The oars were placed in the square oarlocks. The leather bags of food and clothes and seed corn were shoved under the stern deck and wrapped out of the way of the wave-spray. A barrel of water was rolled down and lifted into a place that had been made for it, to hold it upright no matter how the boat rolled.

The posts of Grim's high seat were lashed to the inside of the boat on either side. These had been carved by William Wendut in the days before Grim had been made a thrall. They made a seat of sorts along both sides of the boat. They were too narrow to sleep on, and they crowded into what living space there was. But they were the symbols of Grim's freemanship, and room must be made for them.

One by one Dame Leve, Hugh Raven, and Havelok climbed in and found places in the bottom of the boat beside Gunnild and Levive. The sail was raised and the sheets turned over to Robert the Red. Grim took his place in the bow, bracing himself against the motion of the boat. Pakkanen and William Wendut shoved the boat into deep water and scrambled over the low sides, dripping wet. They found the one seat and picked up the oars.

All of this had been done in a desperate haste, with as few words and as little splashing as they could manage. As the boat rocked away from the shore Hugh Raven saw the sail fill slowly and the oars bite into the placid waters of the firth.

Havelok was watching the high banks of the river. "Look to the south!" he whispered to Hugh Raven.

Hugh Raven twisted around and caught the movement of a horse and rider as they rode up to the cliff's edge, and whirled to ride away.

Grim, too, had seen it. "Find the shields and axes," he called back to William Wendut. "They will send a longboat from Vejle to stop us."

There was not much wind. Robert the Red knew every trick to catch what there was in the big sail, but the boat was heavy laden and low in the water. It seemed as though the black waves rolling by on either side would at any moment come welling over the gunwales.

The rowing had stopped while the men found small iron-bound shields, for the women and boys as well as for themselves. They unfastened the leather casings on the bright axes. These were not battle axes, but the heavy, hard-edged tools men used to build a boat. They looked deadly enough, Havelok was thinking.

Pakkanen had made for himself a stout wooden spear, well-sharpened and fire-hardened. He gave this to Havelok. "Now then, king-born, give a good account of yourself." He picked up a length of wood that had been brought for the thwart braces and hefted it.

Gunnild too picked up one of the heavy wood lengths, but Levive put her pretty face in her mother's lap with a shuddering sob.

When the axes were at hand and the shields fastened to the sides of the boat, William Wendut and Pakkanen put their backs into the rowing. Grim's voice came back to them, barking out the rowing time. The men and the boat answered as though they were a single living thing.

Robert the Red worked his sheets to catch each breath of wind. The small boat took to the sea waves bravely, now up now plunging down, the wave-spray flung back from her curved prow.

Havelok, who did not know as much about boats and the sea as Hugh Raven, had a green taste in his mouth and twinges of deadly sickness. But he was too excited, too much afraid of the pursuers they all knew would soon be beating up the coast on their sea-track, to think much about his queasy stomach.

They were well out on the sea-road in the early dawn, before they saw the pursuit ship.

"She comes!" shouted Grim. "She is a war keel. Change course!"

As the small boat rose on a towering wave they could all see the top of the striped sail far down to the south.

They could not hope to outrun the coming ship, with her sixteen pairs of rowers and her huge billowing sail. But they could tack faster, change course more easily, and keep out of sight longer than the dragon ship.

"If we could reach an island off the coast of Sweden," panted Pakkanen as he swung with his oar, "we could hide behind a headland and ram her. It is a trick of the sea pirates to the south."

Grim nodded. "If we can keep out of sight until dusk," he shouted back, "it is worth trying."

They sailed east then, with a following wind, and soon lost sight of the dragon ship. But by midafternoon they saw the top of the striped sail again, and knew that their change of course had been noted.

"We sail for the first land we can see!" shouted Grim.

By sunset they came upon a small rocky island, thickset and tree-crowned. They beached the boat. The women and the two younger boys fled into the shelter of the forest. Then the boat put off once more, sailing swiftly around the nearest headland.

Havelok and Hugh Raven helped the women find a sheltered spot, deep-hidden by shrubs against a high rock. It was a sun-warmed spot and secret.

"Come on, Hugh Raven," urged Havelok. "Let's climb the hill and watch for the longboat. Maybe we could even see them fight."

"I don't think we s-should," answered Hugh Raven slowly. "I think we s-should s-stay here with my mother and my s-sisters."

Havelok was impatient. "They are as safe here as they will ever be. If our boat is sunk, we will all be rounded up and slain."

Gunnild's dark voice spoke softly. "Havelok is right. Perhaps you can see when our raven boat meets the dragon ship. If our men are killed or captured, the two of you must seek safety away from us. Hide in the trees, or in a cave. Do not try to find us. We will swear that you went down with the boat."

Dame Leve put her arms around the shoulders of the two boys. She pressed her face against first one brown cheek and then the other. Then she pushed them away.

The two boys began the steep climb up the scree to the headland, keeping well down in the shelter of the trees. When they were nearly at the top of the wooded cliffs, they crept up more cautiously, keeping their heads down. It was not until they had reached the topmost ridge, as narrow as a hog's spine, that they could see the longboat coming around the southern tip of the island.

The rowers in Godard's ship were resting on their oars letting the wind work, as though they knew well enough that the small boat they sought must be close at hand. A cluster of fighting men were standing well forward, with drawn swords behind a solid shield-wall.

Water-spurning, the dragon ship came on, cutting through the waves that the smaller boat had ridden up and down like a wood-leaf.

Below the boys, close to the end of the headland, and standing back against the rocks in the dusk, the *Raven of the Winds* looked like a tiny rowboat. Her sail was furled. The men in her had rigged up a second seat of sea-chests, and had put out the extra pair of oars. The two boys could see the ax-gleam between the knees of the rowers.

"I could spit in her from here," said Havelok in a low voice. "I wish there were some way to let them know that the big ship is almost on them."

"We'd better not. They might think that we needed help or s-something. We'd better let them do it as they've

planned. Robert the Red and my father are s-sea-s-skilled."

The Viking ship sailed across the mouth of the little cove where they had let the women out. She stood out to round the streaming, wave-drained rocks of the headland.

Havelok was shaking and hating himself for it. Hugh

Raven clung to a young birch tree hanging out over the edge of the narrow ridge. They watched the dragon prow sail beyond the rocks. Every man on board seemed to be straining his eyes to catch sight of the small boat.

As they sailed past the headland the *Raven of the Winds* swung out of her hiding place. She bore down upon the

Viking ship from the rear. The two men on the right side of the *Raven* shipped their oars. The iron-shod prow of the smaller boat smashed into the spread oars along the side of the longboat. Eight oars were sheered off. The rowers on that side were all knocked in a heap. It happened so fast that the men in Godard's ship scarcely knew what had come upon them.

A man in the small boat sent an ax end over end to strike down the helmsman of the war keel. The larger craft began to drift.

"That was Pakkanen," whispered Hugh Raven in Havelok's ear. "He is deadly with an ax-throw."

Grim's men pushed their boat away from the big ship, as she turned, sore-stricken in the deep sea. Then back the small boat came like a rooster fighting off a fox, smashing into the low side of the dragon ship and driving her helpless into the headland rocks.

Godard's men, thrown to their knees, were struggling to get back to where they could use their axes. The rowers could not get their oars untangled. Two axes were thrown. One landed with a heavy splash in the sea, the other was deep-bedded in the mast of the raven ship above the little silver-wire cross.

As the boys watched from above, the longboat struck on a rock with a hideous smashing of timbers. Half of the men on their feet were tossed into the surging sea.

One man was flung across the side of the smaller boat and dragged himself over the gunwale. One of Grim's sons struck him down with an oar. The rest of Godard's men landed with a crush of arms and legs and weapons in the bottom of the dragon ship. They were struggling to get to their feet as the longboat rose on the next wave and crashed heavily down on the rocks.

In the dim light Havelok and Hugh Raven could see two of the men aboard the small boat rowing as fast and as far as they could. The other two were unfurling the sail. A fifth man, one of Godard's men, lay in a heap in the bottom of the boat. They could see the Dane men who had been flung overboard climbing into the longboat as she listed half in and half out of the water, taking the heavy pounding of the waves.

When Havelok and Hugh Raven looked again the *Raven* was sailing north with her sail full-bellied in the wind.

Havelok flapped his arms and crowed like a young rooster.

Hugh Raven was silent.

"Don't you think it was well planned, this surprise?" asked Havelok, down-daunted by this silence.

"Yes. But we are not free of these men. It is no long s-swim from there to here. Out of all those rowers and a dozen fighting men, a lot of them can s-swim ashore. Anyone of them can ask for anything he wants from Godard, if he can s-say he has killed the lot of us. Do you want your head carried to the Jarl in a s-sack?"

Havelok ran his finger around his neckband. "Well—no. Do you think they know that some of us landed before the fight?"

"I don't know. But they must have s-seen that there were no women in that boat. If Horda is with them, he would know that you were not there. Once off those rocks and on the island, they could follow our tracks. They could find my mother and s-sisters easily enough when they s-see the keel mark on the beach."

"We'd better get down to the shore before they do, then, and brush out the tracks."

Hugh Raven would not hear of this. "It is too dangerous for us to be s-seen by any of Godard's men. But we could go around the other end of the cove, out of sight of the s-ship on the rocks. My father will sail around the island and come back for all of us. We could s-signal to him."

This seemed a good idea to Havelok. "I think Godard's men will stay with their ship, don't you, where they have food and water? If they can get her off at high tide, they might even float her ashore and patch her up. It is the only way they can get home if no one lives on this island."

The two boys slid on their backsides down the steep cliff until they reached easier going. When they came to the part of the woods where the women were hiding they pushed their way through the underbrush. Havelok was whistling as he went, a tune the Finn had sung at the fire.

Gunnild came to meet them. They told her of the trick that had been played on Godard's men, and the wrecking of the dragon ship on the rocks.

Gunnild was unhappy about the two boys going off to wait for the *Raven of the Winds*, but they all knew that it would be unwise for the small boat to come far enough around the island for Godard's men to see her. They would know that Grim's boat had returned for someone on the island. If any of Godard's men had reached shore by that time, it would be easy to track down the women and trap the men as they landed.

So Hugh Raven and Havelok climbed around the cove and south along the shore until they could see Grim's boat returning. Hugh Raven struck sparks with his flint against a lump of iron pyrites onto some dry moss. From this he set a torch of pitch wood blazing.

When the Raven ship was beached the boys led William Wendut to the place where the women were hiding. By the time the short gray hours of a summer night had melted into dawn, all of them were safely aboard the *Raven of the Winds* and south-bound around the island.

To their surprise the boys found an added passenger. One of the men from the dragon ship lay in the bottom of the boat. His eyes were closed. His face behind the straw-colored beard was the color of an unbaked barley cake. The side of his head was swollen with a dark and oozing bruise. His bare arms were covered with writhing patterns of blue tattooing. His head rolled with the motion of the boat and his long, coarse hair, dyed a rusty yellow, was gummed and matted with sea water.

It was Horda, the man Godard had sent to spy on them.

"What is he doing here?" demanded Hugh Raven. He pushed over in the boat to avoid touching the wounded man.

Grim looked down at the sodden, swollen face. "He fell into our boat from the dragon ship. We thought we had killed him. When we came to throw him out we found he was still living."

"We should have finished it then," growled Robert the Red. "We are fools if we don't. All we have to do is to toss him in the sea."

"We are too close to the island," answered Grim. "We must take him out too far away for him to swim back to them, or for a fishing boat to carry him back."

"Why?" demanded Robert the Red.

"We cannot risk it. Horda told Pakkanen that he had known Birkabeyn. He followed Havelok and Hugh Raven into the woods. He knows that Havelok is Birkabeyn's son. We have questioned him here. It is hard to understand his thick speech, but he swears he has not told Godard. Probably because he first hoped to get money from me, for tongue-silence."

"He would have told," said Robert the Red, "as soon as the money was gone."

"The Jarl does not know for sure that Birkabeyn's son is still living," said Grim. "Once he learns that Havelok is alive, he will send men after him to kill him. We must keep Horda from the rest of Godard's men, so they cannot carry the word about the king's son to the Jarl."

"Horda cannot tell anyone if he is dead," argued Robert the Red. "If we kill him and throw him overboard, he cannot tell anyone anything."

"You cannot do that, my son," said Dame Leve. "This man came to us as a gift of Wyrd, the Fate Goddess. We cannot refuse that gift."

Through all this talk Horda lay in the bottom of the boat, close enough for any of them to touch. Whether he was too ill with head-pain to talk, or feigning a sort of death-sleep and so learn what fate they had in mind for him, no one could tell.

William Wendut braced himself against the gunwale behind Robert the Red who was rowing. He yawned mightily. "Give me two hours' sleep and then waken me."

Dame Leve pulled Levive's bright head onto her shoulder. "You, too, my daughter, sleep now. The dragon peril is behind us. I will watch to see if this Godard's man should stir."

"That's another thing," grumbled Robert the Red. "At least one of us must watch him every minute. The sea is not the greatest danger to us." His hands were impatient on the sheets and the small boat bucked as the wind caught her. "It is an ill omen for this journey of ours, having this man in our boat."

Pakkanen shook his head. "I think we are in luck. It is far better that Horda goes with us than back to Godard with the news of the king's son."

"I am sure that Wyrd meant it to be good fortune for us," said Dame Leve firmly.

"Ar–r–r!" growled Robert the Red.

vii

The Death Ship

By midmorning the wind had dropped. Ahead of them lay a solid bank of fog, low-reaching, hugging the water. It had the heavy curdled look of wool on a sheep's back.

As the boat plunged into the murk the sail hung slack, flapping wetly against the mast. The only other sounds were the splash and dip of the oars, the squeak of the oar locks and the chug and thump of sullen waves as they met the iron prow of the *Raven*.

"What if we lose our way," asked Havelok, "and come back to the island?"

"We shall not lose our way," said William Wendut. "Grim could take us north through the water itself."

The crew took turns sleeping and rowing. Dame Leve and Gunnild took turns sleeping and keeping watch over the prone figure of Horda. Hugh Raven rowed for a while, but Havelok had never used oars and he was more trouble than he was worth.

There was a dreamlike quality to the heaving boat, moving with disheartening slowness through the mist. All on board were drenched. Those not rowing huddled together under the clammy skins they dragged out from beneath the stern. Their food of cold, dried fish and the hard, twice-baked bread did little to warm them. Dame Leve took her food and crushed some of it against the gunwale. She moistened this with a little of the sour wine in a big skin bottle, and pressed it between the cracked lips of Horda.

She drank but little of her cup of water. The rest she tilted between his parted lips. He gulped it down, stirring and turning with a deep groan.

"We may have need of every drop of water and wine before we see Norway," growled Robert the Red. "Let him be. There will soon be water enough in the sea to quench his thirst."

Dame Leve paid no attention. She folded a square of thick woolen stuff. She lifted Horda's head from the ship boards, and the sloshing water in the bottom of the boat, onto this makeshift pillow.

For two days they rowed, taking turns. Even Gunnild asked them to let her take a turn at the rowing. "I grow stiff and sadly cramped with this sitting," she complained. "Let me stretch my long legs and work the knots from my shoulders at the same time."

Havelok watched her as she bent forward to catch the stroke. Gunnild was not as pretty as Levive, he was thinking, but she moved in a kind of serenity that had a beauty of its own. It was like looking into the hazel waters of a trout pool to look into the quiet eyes of Gunnild Grimsdatter. Her beauty was bone-deep.

On the third day Horda sat up in the boat. His face

was pasty, except for the ugly blue and green bruise on the side of his head that had blacked and shut one eye.

"You are better now?" asked Dame Leve.

"I am sick and dizzy," he growled. "My head is ringing like a war-shield, and I am as hungry as a wolf."

"You have a tough skull to stand such a blow," said William Wendut, swinging back and forth as he rowed through the mist.

Horda's one good eye squinted into one face and then the other. He wiped away the fog droplets from the untidy beard that flowed down around his loose lips. When he shifted his body to ease his cramped muscles, the iron rings of his byrnie clinked and jingled.

Grim wakened at the sound. He peered ahead beneath the brim of the tight skin hat that he wore. "It will fair up tomorrow," he told them. "Even now you can see the light in the west where the sun travels across the sky."

Havelok stared into the fog. It all seemed gray-blind and dismal. His bones ached with rolling on the bottom of the boat. He had a crick in his neck from the way he had slept curled around Hugh Raven's feet.

Grim handed to each of them a small share of dried fish and the hard biscuit. Again Dame Leve offered half of hers to Horda.

He took it and wolfed it down with no word of thanks. "What would you do with me?" he asked of Grim.

Grim eyed him for a full minute of time. Robert the Red had wakened too. He sat shoving his fingers through his soaking wet hair, shaking his head like a wet dog.

"We are far enough from the island now, so you could

not get back," Grim told Horda. "I had agreed to carry you just so long."

"We are past the narrows and into the north sea," whined Horda. "If you throw me into the sea now, fisherman, I cannot win back to land by any means. It is too far to swim. No boat would see me in this cursed fog."

"We have no food to spare for a traitor's mouth," said Robert the Red.

"Quiet, puppy," ordered Grim.

Horda's malicious little eye swiveled around to meet Robert the Red's glare. He turned back to Grim. "See, then. I will make a bargain with you. Carry me in this boat until you have a landfall. Set me on the beach with enough food for three days—"

"That is fair enough," said Pakkanen.

"Yes," agreed Dame Leve. "Wyrd will not turn against us for that."

"Why should we?" shouted Robert the Red. "He would have killed us or betrayed us to Godard."

Horda ignored him. "Here is my bargain. I owe Godard nothing. I am a freeman. If you give me this chance at life, I promise to give Godard no word of the cargo you carry to Norway. If not—" his one eye glittered, "I will win through somehow, to Vejle. I will bring Godard tidings that will set a dozen berserkers on the trail of the king's son."

Grim pulled at his moustache. He ran his calloused fingers over the rough gray hair growing down around his ears. "What is the security you give for this?"

Horda plucked a long hair from his yellow beard. "By the hair of Thor's beard—"

"You cannot take the word of this heathen, Grim!" protested Robert the Red.

Horda leaned forward and wrapped the hair around the arm of the little wire cross on the mast. "I will swear by your cross then," he said, "or both."

"I will think on this," said Grim.

The next day the fog lightened. They could see the ocean swells fifty feet in front of the *Raven's* head. There was air enough astir to raise the sail. Robert the Red cupped it to catch the slightest breath of wind. The sun hung like a pale shield-disk as the fog thinned.

"We can soon see land now," said Horda when he wakened. "Will you set me ashore if it lies on either hand, Grim?"

"Yes."

Dame Leve smiled happily. She again offered part of her food ration to Horda. He swallowed it as a dog swallows, in one gulp. He offered no more thanks than before.

By noon the wind was coming in strong puffs, driving the fog before it in tatters and shreds. Not too long before midnight they could see the sunset colors of the clouds, salmon-pink and gold.

In the middle of the night when a well-worn moon was rising, the fog lifted and the moonlight lay in a long, shimmering bar over the heaving water. The three of them who were awake, Robert the Red and Havelok and Pakkanen, could see as far as the horizon on both sides of them. A low bank of clouds hid the way ahead.

There was no land on either side of the boat. The water seemed to Havelok to stretch to the end of the world. Fear gripped him. He thought of the terrors waiting for them where the sea stopped and there was nothing ahead, neither land nor water. He felt himself falling—falling—and jerked himself awake.

Pakkanen was staring ahead. Out of the cloud bank he could see something. It was something that moved and seemed to spread dark wings over the sea as it came toward them, swinging up and down with the rise and fall of the waves.

"Grim!" shouted Robert the Red.

Grim and all the rest were instantly awake. Grim crawled slowly past the crouching people in the boat, his old muscles stiff and sore from his hard bed. He hung onto the curved prow with both hands as the boat lifted to meet a rising wave and slid down into the following trough.

The wind was blowing hard now, catching the spindrift from the foaming crests, blowing white plumes like smoke ahead of the breaking waves.

William Wendut unstrapped his ax. Pakkanen caught up his long spear. All of them stared at the thing ahead that rode the waves so clumsily.

"It is a ship," Grim called back. "A black ship that wallows in the sea."

Now they could all see that it was a ship, a ship that dipped and plunged in the water, lurching and staggering as she struggled forwards or backwards when the waves caught her. She was a long ship, as long as a Danish war keel. Her sail of shining silk had a great cross emblazoned on it, of red and blue and gold. This cross had all four ends split and curled back, as though the painter had meant it to be both pagan and Christian. The sail had been partially burned and hung limp and blackened from the crossarm.

There was no life aboard the black ship. Only death. Bound on a high wooden throne that was painted in bright colors, there sat an upright figure, richly dressed. On his head there shone a square-cut crown. At his feet were stacked boxes and bales, and the bones of dead horses and dogs.

From over the sides of the black ship trailed long loops of black cloth, rusty and tattered and dragging in the sea.

"A death ship!" whispered Pakkanen. "A king's ship of death."

They could see, as the black ship drew on, the branches and cut wood that were stacked at the feet of the dead king. These too were partially burnt.

"A rain storm must have doused the fire," said Grim, "that was meant to burn and sink the ship."

"Where has it come from?" asked Gunnild in a trembling voice.

"Who knows," answered Pakkanen, "where it has come from or how long it has traveled the sea-road? Perhaps it comes from Ireland, or from the islands north of the Picts."

"Or from the land at the end of the world," said William Wendut.

A dread silence fell upon the boatload of people staring at the king's ship.

"God was good to us," whispered Gunnild, "that we did not meet it in the fog. For surely we would have all gone down." She crossed herself and shuddered.

William Wendut was working his oar like a rudder trying to turn the *Raven of the Winds* to avoid the wash of the death ship. As they drew nearer they could hear something thumping and thudding inside the ship. The dead king had his head lowered and turned a little to one side under the heavy crown. It was as though he were listening to this noise, and puzzled by it.

The two ships drew closer together. "Haul in! Haul in!" shouted William Wendut. "She will sink us if she rams us."

They were close enough now to see the face of the dead king. It was a death's head, a skull with the flesh gone from it. Only the hair was still flowing from under the crown and blowing in the wind. They could not see his hands because broad leather bands bound them to the arms of the high throne. His feet were covered with death shoes to speed him on his journey.

There was a sudden splash. They whirled about. A head bobbed out of the sea, and they saw it was Horda's. Struck dumb, they watched him swim with quick, powerful strokes of one arm, toward the black ship. The other arm was around something bulky that helped to hold him up.

"There will be a dread curse upon him!" wailed Dame Leve. "Come back!" she called.

"Let him go!" shouted Robert the Red. "Let the dead king have him!"

Horda turned his head as he reached for one of the black drapes hanging in the sea. Now they could see that in his other arm he carried their skin of sour wine. It buoyed him up when the waves pushed by the boat.

"This is better than land," he shouted at them. "There will be food in the lockers." He began to pull himself over the gunwale of the heaving, plunging ship. "Because of Dame Leve I will keep your secret." The wind carried some of his words away, but they heard the last of it plainly enough. "I will dance at your crowning, king's son."

The wind freshened and tugged at their own sail. Robert the Red let it fill. The boat gathered way, speeding past the death ship in a sort of panic flight from the very sight and sound of it.

When they were past, the longship with the burned sail seemed to steady herself, as though a hand on her helm had given her stability and direction. They watched her as long as she was in sight. Only when the longboat melted into the velvet night, could they turn from watching, and sleep.

In the night the wind rose. The *Raven of the Winds* scudded before it. The waves slapped into the boat. All of them, except Robert the Red who tightened or slackened his sail as the wind shifted, fell to bailing out sea water with anything they could find at hand, from a leather helmet to a clay cup.

The wind was from the north and east. It drove them past the coast of Norway like a chip in a mountain freshet. They could see the rough rocks of a fiord, but they could not see where they could make a landing in the high seas.

The waves smashed down on the prow and under it. They raced away behind the boat, slopping over the gunwales enough to keep those in the boat bailing out the sea water.

"Shall we try to win back?" shouted Robert the Red as he fought the straining sail. "When this blow has spent itself?"

"It might be wise to go on to the west," said Grim. "Those behind us think we mean to land in Norway. We have tricked them once, why not again?"

"I had thought to go to Norway," said Pakkanen, laughing. "But there is time enough."

"We will follow where the wind drives then," said Grim. "To the west lies England, land of the Angles."

"If Horda tells Godard that Havelok lives," said Robert the Red with a short laugh, "his men will look long in Norway for Birkabeyn's son."

"We cannot speak this English tongue!" moaned Dame Leve.

"I can," said Pakkanen.

"We can learn it," said Robert the Red.

The days were long as they fought the wind. The food lockers were nearly empty. The fresh water was almost unfit to drink, and almost gone as well. Grim put out lines, but the fish they caught were too spiny to give them more than a few bones to suck. There was a bitter whip to the wind-blast. The salt water flung in their faces was colder than snow.

"I have s-sat in puddles of ice-water until my clothes are rotting off," said Hugh Raven in Havelok's ear.

Havelok held up a single leather shoe, soggy and slimy. "What good is it, putting it on?"

"Wear them," said Grim shortly. "Wet or dry, you will need them for the rocks."

"What rocks?" muttered Havelok. But he was careful to keep his words for Hugh Raven's ear alone.

Grim was short of temper now, with his own aches and pains, and the worry he ate and slept with. He was heavy-handed when he lashed out. It did not pay to anger him. Even Levive had felt the back of his hand, when she had wept aloud in her hunger and misery.

Over all of them had settled a savage and merciless sense of impending doom. Even William Wendut had lost his ready laugh. Grim pulled in his belt against the hunger pains that racked him, sitting hunched against the bitter wind.

At times Pakkanen sang songs to them to lighten their mood. He told them strange tales of the old Norse gods. He could not play his harp, because the strings would not hold a tune, but he sang long Kalevala verses and told them stories of the beginnings of things.

"Have you heard how Seeland came to be?" He would

ask. His voice carried above the whistle of the wind. They huddled in the boat, hugging their belts to still their gnawing hunger.

"Once upon a far-off time a king named Gyle, of Svithjod, gave to a wayfaring woman who had pleased him with her storytelling, a plowland in his realm. As large, he told her, as four oxen could plow in a day and a night. She was of the Asa race and her name was Gefjon. She journeyed to Jotunnheim to find the four sons of a giant and her. These she changed into four great oxen, curly-browed and deep-chested, fierce-eyed and splay-footed. She set them before the plow. Then went the plow so hard, so deep that it tore up the land and the oxen drew it into the sea. Until it stood still with water on four sides of it. There Gefjon set the land she had plowed. From where the land had been ravaged there was naught but sea. And Gefjon's land she called Seeland."

Havelok could see that great giant of a woman striding behind her huge, straining oxen, and the deep plow tearing up the land from the sea. He could see the water sheeting out on either side of the plowshare. For a while he could forget his hunger in the wonder of it.

One afternoon with the wind beating at the sail and the boat heeling as she fled before it, Dame Leve spoke out in her clear voice. "We are Dane folk. They are long enduring."

Later before the sun set, a wind-beaten gull lighted on the mast top. It gave its creaking cry, mouth agape and wings widespread for balance, as the mast swung with the push and drive of the wind.

Pakkanen lifted his face to the bird. "A gull is a land bird," he said.

The next day they sighted the east coast of England.

"We shall go north," said Grim, his voice ringing with relief, "to the first river mouth. If it does not seem a good place to put down roots, we can at least fill our water barrel with fresh water, and perhaps buy food to take us up the coast."

As if to welcome them the sun shone out from behind the clouds, and the wind slackened. To their sea-tired eyes England looked green and beautiful.

viii

The New Land

As they sailed north with the land on their left, Pakkanen got out the little bone kantele. He tuned it in the sunshine and sang to them in his high chanting voice:

> "Then the aged Väinämöinen
> Answered in the words which follow:
> 'There is wonder after wonder;
> There's a pine with flowery summit,
> Flowery summit, leaves all golden,
> . . . .
> On the crown the moon is shining,
> In the boughs the Bear is resting.'"

"It is strange how you find words that fit the time," said Gunnild. "Words like 'the crown' and 'the Bear' could easily be about Havelok, whom we named Bjorn, the Bear."

"That is the beauty of most of the epics," Pakkanen said. "There are words for every mood, every time, all people."

By noon they had reached a large river mouth which had formed a great bay leading into the land. The water of the firth made a brownish stain a long way out into the sea.

"From the silt it brings down, this is a big river," said Grim. "Let us sail up this stream and see what we find."

With a breeze behind them they sailed up the broad reaches of the bay. It was calmer water here. The small waves sucked and clucked below the *Raven's* breast and ran in shallow breakers along the brown sands. To the south they could see low hills, forest-crowned. The shores to north and south of them were low-lying and dim, with long stretches of sand and mud flats and salt grass.

"This is tide water," said Grim, dipping his fingers in the water and sucking them. "We must sail far enough inland to find sweet water."

"Do we look to the north bank or the south, Grim?" asked Robert the Red.

"To the south. We shall be safer there from the Pictish raids."

Several miles inland, to the south, they could see some chalk cliffs where a deep stream had dug for itself a passage to the river.

"Good enough?" asked William Wendut.

"Good enough," answered Grim.

Havelok kneeled in the boat, his face to the new land, his heart beating. It was hard to believe they had come safely to the end of the flight from Denmark. It had seemed, at the last, as though it must go on forever.

Robert the Red furled the sail. William Wendut and Pakkanen took the oars to guide the boat into the fresh-water stream. Grim stayed at the prow, a leather helmet on his head, a short spear in his hand. They moved slowly, keeping the boat in the shadows, watching the shores for strange faces. They listened for a challenge, or the twang of a bowstring, the clunk of a slung stone.

Once out of the ocean waves the boat settled on the mirrored water like a seagull floating. The shores were full of seabirds that rose with clattering wings and raucous cries, as the boat moved slowly upstream.

Behind the creek shores lay the wildwood where the hills were thick with oak and beech trees and pines. Below the woods there were flowery meadows with knee-deep grass, golden-ripe, and tall fragile poppies red as blood.

"There are birds to snare, fish to catch, and feed-grass for cattle," said Grim. "The soil looks black and fertile. Shall we stay here?"

All of them, tired of the sea, weary of wet clothes and little food and water, sick of the biting, cutting wind, sighed at the very thought of it, and gladly agreed.

They sailed slowly up the stream, testing its depth. Beyond a bend they came upon a small settlement of clay and wattle huts. A few dogs barked at them. Some bony cows raised their heads from their grazing to stare at them. A handful of black-haired children playing half-naked at the water's edge, scuttled off to the shelter of the huts.

No one hailed them. Since the water still had depth they went farther up the creek out of sight of the huts. They found a level meadow starred with flowers. An earlier bank of the stream would be at their backs against the winter snow and wind. There was a small sandy cove where they could beach their boat.

William Wendut fell to his knees on the packed sand of the curved beach. "Hail Mary, Mother of Christ," he cried, "Who hast brought us safe across the sea—"

It was good to feel earth beneath their feet again, but it was hard to get used to after the motion of the boat.

Havelok thought he had never tasted anything so delicious as the clear, sweet water in the brook, after the stale and crawling water in the barrel. He thought that even in Denmark he had never seen any countryside more beautiful than this river valley, where the oaks and beeches marched down to the river. The open places were sweet with meadow flowers. The greens of grass and tree were greener than any green he had ever seen.

There came an upsurge of happiness for all of them. No matter what this new land had to offer, they had won through to it. They had tricked the dragon ship and shaken off the pursuit of Godard's men. They had lost Horda to the death ship, without bringing down the wrath of Wyrd on their own heads. Even if Horda returned to Denmark and told Godard of Havelok, they were a whole land away from Norway where it was thought they had gone.

For a while they sat beneath the trees, in a kind of giving over to the end of the long, hard voyage. Grim added his own heartfelt prayer, "God speed our boat and plow, and give us fish and corn enow."

By noon Grim had set them all to work, except Havelok and Pakkanen.

Hugh Raven was to unload the boat and get all the things under cover of trees or skins, until they could build a shelter.

Robert the Red and William Wendut were to get wood

for two fires, one small one for cooking, a larger one for warmth and the drying of clothes. Then they were to help Grim with the boat.

Levive and Gunnild were to see to the wet clothes and what food they had. Dame Leve was to make up beds of sorts under the trees, in the lee of the overturned boat, in any sheltered spots.

"I shall keel the boat and scrape the weeds and barnacles from her hull," said Grim. "We must spread the sail and go over it for any tender places in the thread. If we have need to escape from this place, the boat must be seaworthy."

"And I?" asked Pakkanen.

Grim looked at him from under his gray brows. "You are not of my clan, Finn. Nor of my household. You more than earned your way on my boat. I have no further claim on your labors."

Pakkanen laughed. "Shall I just sit here, then, and watch you work? Set me a task, Grim. There's enough work here for another pair of hands." His eyes went slantwise to where Havelok sat in a sort of daydream on a bleached log. "For both of us, eh, Havelok?"

Havelok came out of his trance. "I can help, too," he said, a little uncertainly.

Grim pulled at his moustache and thought about this. "Since you speak the language of these people, Finn, will you go to the nearest town and learn where we are? Could you find out to whom we are beholden? Also find out whether we can stay here on this river peaceably? It seems to me better that we go to these people and ask these things with good intent, than that they come to us in anger. Or worse yet, go to their men of power and complain of our trespass. So?"

"Yes. Let me take the two youngest with me. I will help them unload the boat and turn it before we go. No one will think me hostile with a pair of puppies like these two in tow."

Grim nodded. "It will stretch their legs."

"Pull this over your hair then, Bjorn," said Gunnild. She handed Havelok a skin cap to pull down below his ears. "It's a strange head of hair you have now," she teased. "Rusty black on top and golden at the roots. We don't want people asking questions about a boy with dyed hair."

"I'll tell them I fell into a tanning vat," said Havelok.

The two boys were well pleased to be going to the next town, no matter how far or how near it might be. They changed into dry clothes. As soon as the boat was empty and careened on the sands, they set out with Pakkanen along the track that led over the moors.

The Finn asked the first sheepherder they came to about the nearest town. Afterwards he told the boys what the man had said. "The river we have sailed up is the Humber. It lies well to the north of England. The land is under the rule of Godrich, the Earl of Cornwall. This man is not of royal stock, but holds the land in fee for the daughter of Athelwold, the last king. She is a little maid, less than six summers now, and too young to rule. Later she will be England's queen, if Godrich keeps his death promise to the old king. It is easy to see he is feared, this Godrich."

It came to Havelok's thinking that this princess was no

better off than he had been, if this English Earl chose to be as treacherous as Jarl Godard.

"What of the town?" asked Havelok. "Is it near or far?"

"It is too far to go today. Lincoln is the closest town and it will take us two days to come and go."

The two boys were disappointed. They were afraid that Grim would not let them go if it would take so long.

"Earl Godrich is not there," Pakkanen said. "But his business is done by a shire reeve who collects his rents. The sheepherder tells me that Grim can probably gain the right to live and fish and raise a herd here, if he will swear fealty to Earl Godrich, pay his taxes in money or kind, and fight with the Earl against raiders from abroad, or else the Scots."

"So it is in Denmark," said Havelok.

"Do we go or stay, then?" asked Hugh Raven.

"That is for Grim to settle. I think it will help if I see the shire reeve and clear these matters with him. It would make it easier for Grim. Without this there might be some resentment because you are Danish folk. Along this coast there is still fear of the Danes because of the land-raiding in past years. When he knows you are fisherfolk and not raiders, probably the Earl will let you stay. He has a nose for rents, this Earl."

They started back across the country. Pakkanen strode ahead, using his sharpened wooden spear as a staff. He had a short knife with him, in a fur scabbard hanging from his belt. The two boys each had a stout stick.

There were fleecy clouds in the blue sky, and the heather hummed with bees. Sometimes the track lay through the open fields, turning this way and that to miss the marshy spots along a stream. Again it plunged into the woodland, beneath oaks and alders and beeches where the way was cool and dark with shade. On the upland wold there were shallow ponds where geese and ducks swam, or made their way roundabout, to nests hidden in the bushes.

It was warm walking in the sun. The gorse had a hot and dusty smell, but in the woods there was the breath of pines and a grass-scent, cool and woodsy. How different, Havelok was thinking, was the smell of the earth from the smell of the sea.

The boys galloped here and there to see everything at once. Pakkanen let them go, whistling on his fingers to call them back if they ranged too far afield. Havelok was like a wild thing turned loose. Behind him were the bitter days of his imprisonment, the worried time with Grim when he must hide or play the clod, and the weeks in a plunging boat at sea.

Now he had come to a new land, a new life. He was no longer Havelok, King of Denmark, or a hunted fugitive from the treachery of Godard. He was the foster son of Grim, a fisherman, newly come to a green and beautiful land. He was the brother of Hugh Raven. There would be time enough later to be King of Denmark.

Besides this, he had seen a white horse on the road and had spit over his little finger. A white horse meant good luck as any Dane knew, because of Odin's eight-legged horse Sleipnir, who could outrun the wind.

They were glad to get to bed before the summer sun had set, happy because Grim had agreed to let them go the following two days. They were up and off in the early morning hours, with dried fish and the hard ship's bread as their only fare.

They met charcoal burners who asked them for news. The Finn had little enough to tell, but he embroidered what he had so that it seemed new and fresh to them.

They caught up with a peddler's wain, a broad-wheeled cart with a cover of thick, dark cloth over bent willow withes. Walking beside the flea-bitten donkey that drew it was a wall-eyed peddler. He walked a little way with them and stopped at a wood-track leading steeply to a sod hut.

The hut sat against a red-brown cliff stained with the dark drip of water from a rusty spring, and furred over with delicate green grasses. Beside the house they could see the bee skeps covered with ancient, blackened thatch.

"She has no money, this carline," explained the peddler, "and I think perhaps she is a witchcraft woman. But she bakes a crusty loaf of bread and she has pots of berry jam, sweeter than honey."

Havelok licked his lips. He was remembering the sweet comb honey he and Hugh Raven had brought home from the bee tree. Suddenly he was ravenously hungry.

"I'm s-starved!" said Hugh Raven.

Pakkanen reached somewhere about his person, and brought out a silver penny. "Would she sell us bread and jam for this?" he asked.

"She would sell her soul for it," said the peddler. "And for half that much I'll get you a loaf and a pot of jam to take home with you. For the rest here are leather laces to tie up your clothes, and a ribbon for your pretty one's hair. And the rest for me, good sirs, for my trouble, eh?"

Pakkanen pursed his lips. "Only if you get us a whole loaf

of bread and another ribbon. We have two pretty ones at home. One ribbon will not stretch between them."

"Here are your laces and your ribbons," agreed the peddler. "But I cannot promise the bread until we see if the old woman will part with it."

They hurried up the path to the sod hut where there was a sweet cool smell from the violet bed by the door. An old dog all bones and mangy hair rose to sniff at their hands and heels. He flopped back again in the dappled shade.

The old woman was as brown as a nut and wrinkled as a withered berry after frost. She greeted them with a rune sign she made with a skinny finger in the air. She gave them slices of bread and jam. When they had eaten and given her all the news they had, she sold them a loaf of fresh-baked bread and a small clay pot of the thick, black sweet.

She would have kept them there, hungry as she was for talk. But Pakkanen hurried them away. "We have a long way to go," he told her," and must find a place to stay by dark. We are strangers here, newcomers, and we would be way-lost by nightfall."

She told them of a farm house where they could stay. "If you must have a bed, it will cost you something. If you are willing to sleep in the straw, it will cost you nothing, and the man will give you milk for your supper, if you will do the milking."

She begged them to come back. "Look! I can tell you what the three Fates are weaving for you." She caught up Havelok's hand and bent down to peer at the lines in it.

She turned it this way and that. She pulled the cap from his head and stared at the rooted gold of his hair.

"Two stars in this hand," she muttered. "I have never

yet seen even one star in any hand I have scanned. And a head of hair dark-dyed but springing gold. Who are you, boy?"

"I am Havelok, son of Grim," he said stoutly.

"That's not all of it," she said sharply. "No one can have two stars in their hand, unless—"

Pakkanen pushed them ahead of him down the steep track. They went through the woods chewing happily on thick slices of crusty bread thick-spread with berry jam. They felt rich. They had bread and jam, two ribbons, and a handful of laces to sweeten their homecoming.

Lincoln was a city of wattle huts, some log houses, a few of stone. To Hugh Raven it seemed a huge place, full of noise and filth and confusion. He stared about him. Hurrying up this street and down that were more people than he had ever seen at once. There were friars and monks and students. Carters drove by with loads of wood, vegetables, filled sacks. Men carried wicker cages with chickens and geese, and a stout country woman waddled by with a squealing pig beneath her arm. Merchants in fur-trimmed gowns and urchins nearly naked jostled each other in the street.

To Havelok, who had lived in a city all of his short life, this seemed a small enough town. Vejle he remembered as a fairer place, full of light with more houses of stone, and a fair-carven church beside the king's mound.

As they made their way through the narrow, muddy streets, skirting clumps of cow dung and the open gutters running down the center of the streets, where people threw their slops to the pigs stretched out in the mud, Havelok pinched his nose against the smells. He was remembering the streets of Vejle where the steps of the houses were washed and swept, and the pigs and cattle penned.

A wave of homesickness for Denmark swept over him.

The Shire Reeve was a huge man with eyes that started from his head, and a chuckle that set his cheeks to wobbling. Yes, they could stay on the coast where they were camped. Of course he must send word to Earl Godrich who had the last say in these matters. The Earl would send for Grim, and, yes, for Pakkanen too, if Grim had no other tongue than Danish.

Yes, they could cut any soft wood for housing, but no oak or other hard wood without permission of the Earl. No, they could not hunt, Earl Godrich was strict about the deer . . . but—the Reeve winked at Pakkanen—"A hare now and then, or a brace of birds will never be missed."

Pakkanen left silver on the table when they left. Havelok knew that Grim must have given him money, so that all would be smooth in the dealings with the Shire Reeve and the Earl.

They stopped in the stalls along the river long enough to buy corn and a greasy slab of hogback. These Pakkanen wrapped in the same cloth sack that held the bread and the small pot of jam.

The two boys were hungry again, but Pakkanen let them whistle for it. They looked hopefully at the sack that held the bread and the dark sweet, but the Finn shouldered the sack and set off through the gates at a sharp pace. The boys followed glumly enough and were hard put to it to keep up with him.

"Dark is no time for a leg-walker to be caught on strange roads," Pakkanen called back to them. "Bread and meat is a good excuse to slit a man's throat."

They kept up with him after that. A few miles out of Lincoln they came to the farm of the man the old woman had said might put them up. He was willing to let them sleep in the hayloft and, when Pakkanen had sung for the family, he and the boys were given a barley cake apiece and a mug of milk warm from the cow.

The rest of the way home seemed far shorter than the way to Lincoln had been. A few furlongs from the beach they met William Wendut, ax in hand, striding along the track through the woods.

"No, all is well at the beach," he told them. "But it is good to know that you are nearly home. The camp is well set up. I have even had time to catch two fat salmon for supper."

"Fish!" cried Hugh Raven. "Just wait—"

Pakkanen kicked him sharply on the ankle.

In sight of the camp the whole family welcomed them with shouts. It was plain to see that Grim and the rest had been concerned and worried for their safety in this strange new land.

The ribbons and leather thongs were received with cries of pleasure. There were tears of joy when Pakkanen brought out the corn and meat. But there was a stunned silence when they first saw the bread and jam.

"It's been so long!" cried Levive, hugging the little clay pot of jam up under her chin. "I am so sick and wearied of old, dried fish!"

"It is a good thing that you added the word 'dried' to

that," said William Wendut, his round face rueful. "It seems that I was overly pleased at my two fat fish from the river."

Grim bent a stern look on his younger daughter. "It will be an ill time for us when a good catch of fish will not be welcome in this house."

"I didn't mean it!" cried Levive, abashed. "Truly I. . . ." She held the jam pot out to William Wendut. "Here, take it."

William took the round pot from his sister. "For your scorn of my catch I get your share, is that it?"

She nodded unhappily. William Wendut laughed. He clasped her fingers around the little clay jar. "Be of good cheer, greedy one. A single bite of your share would stick in my throat like a hen bone."

At Levive's long-drawn sigh all of them shouted with laughter.

Havelok was thinking that he had never heard this whole family laughing together, since he had come among them. He knew then the heavy burden of fear they had carried with them, seeking safety for their king, willing to give up home and country to come this long, far, dangerous way.

There was a feast that night on the beach, by the light of the fire. The fresh fish stew was hot and savory. The bread and jam were sweeter even than the boys remembered from the day before.

Afterwards Pakkanen picked out a few tunes on his harp, tunes like little ripples of laughter. But the boys were too tired to listen. Havelok crept under a fur robe beside Hugh Raven on the beach in the lee of the tilted boat, his feet to the fire. The sand made a hard bed with no give to it, like turf or pine needles would have had. But nothing except a raid could have kept either of the boys awake.

Havelok was bone-tired and muscle-sore. But his stomach was full of good food, he was safe with his foster family from the perils of the sea. They could stay in this haven they had found.

The solid earth made for better sleeping than an open, pitching boat.

ix

The Fledgling Hawks

The next day Grim chose a place above the river with a long view both up and down stream. He set his older sons to work cutting sod into squares for a house. It would be a small house to begin with, a place to sleep and a shelter for their seed corn. It would do for a stable later when there were beasts to house.

"We have little enough to put in it now," said Grim, "but with God's help and our own hard work, we shall have more."

Gunnild and Levive went into the woods a little way to find what berries the birds might have left. Dame Leve followed the small stream close by the house-building place, to hunt for water cress or other greens, or bulbs that would nourish them and flavor the plain food caught in the sea or trapped.

Hugh Raven went to work stacking the sods his brothers cut, and Pakkanen helped them.

Havelok sat by the boat.

He had expected Hugh Raven to stay with him, or to

go off into the woods, as they had done most days together in Denmark. He felt lonesome, left out and in some way abused. He kicked at the sand and scowled at the builders.

Pakkanen straightened to ease his back. He glanced down the beach to where Havelok sat and glowered. "It seems to me," he said to Grim, as they both walked down to the small stream for a drink, "that our young kinglet is bored. Have you no work for him? It makes a long day for a boy when he has nothing to do."

"He is a king's son," answered Grim, lowering himself full length to plunge his hands and arms in the cold, clear water. He put his head down to get a drink and came up with his long moustache running rivers of water, like an old walrus. "I cannot order him about as I do my own. Besides—he is clumsy. He does not know how to use tools."

"He will never learn unless you teach him. He is not here in England with you on a visit. Nor yet for a few weeks. It will be years before he can fight Godard for his kingdom. Is he, being king-born, to sit idle for ten or twelve years, then?"

"What can he do? You and Hugh Raven can stack sods faster than we can cut them."

"Almost anything will do that he can see is worth the doing. Set him to work cleaning and polishing your weapons with a piece of woolen stuff and some sand. He can do them no harm. He might even shine them up for you. Have him bring them to the house place where he can talk and joke with us."

At first, when Grim suggested this, Havelok was angry. "That is churl's work," he said, curtly.

Grim shrugged and would have let the matter go, but the Finn took a hand in it.

"So is hunting and fishing for the king's table, Bear cub. Unless you choose to do it. When you choose, then it is a sport. A king has trainers for his hawks, but he also trains them and flies them himself, no?"

"But—" began Havelok.

"Every man cherishes the tools he works with," the Finn added, "and the weapons he fights with. Perhaps you forget that Grim's weapons are your weapons, king's son." Pakkanen turned away to go back to his work, and Grim with him. "The weapons are under the sailcloth," he said over his shoulder.

For some time Havelok sat where he was, kicking at the sand. Then he sauntered over to the humped up sailcloth and lifted one corner. At the edge of the pile there was a knife in a leather casing, a knife with a handle of reindeer horn. He drew it out and noted the rusty-red sea-stain on the iron. "What do I clean it with?" he asked Pakkanen.

"A wad of tow from a frayed rope or a bit of wool. Wet it in fish oil and then in sand."

"What happened after the Sampo was lost, Pakkanen?" asked Hugh Raven.

"A–ah!" The Finn stacked one square of sod against another. "There was now no more magic mill to grind out riches and salt—"

Havelok was scrubbing for dear life and listening with both ears.

With so many working at it, the house was finished in a few days. There were no windows. The door was hung with sewn skins. On either side of the door stood the tall carved posts they had brought from Denmark. A huge driftwood log with strange silver twists that showed it to be a far-traveled wood had been squared and laid across the top of the two posts. The roof was of fir poles with a thick layer of thatch held down by heather ropes with round sea rocks knotted into them.

There was a hearth place in the center of the earthen floor, and a smoke hole rigged above it. It was a snug house that would hold out rain and snow, and shade them from the summer sun.

When the house was done they had a feast of hashed porpoise in sauce, and berries from the woodland.

There were sods left over from the house building. The Finn begged the use of these. "I would build us a sauna—a bath house."

"We can bathe in the river," protested Havelok.

"We can finish our bath in the river," said Pakkanen, "or in a snow bank which is better. But we have to bake ourselves first."

The sauna was built on the rocks above the river. It was a tiny house with no windows and a slit of a door with a tight-stretched leather curtain. There was a hearth on one side with a rough chimney of earth and twigs to carry off the smoke. Across from the hearth a high shelf of sods had been built up under the roof.

"Now we need birch twigs with the leaves still on," said Pakkanen.

"What for?" asked Hugh Raven.

Pakkanen answered with a whinny of laughter.

They brought him armloads of twigs. He had built a

roaring fire on the hearth. He set the twigs in a leather bucket of hot water. "Strip!" he ordered.

They peeled off their tunics and shoes. He drove them ahead of him into the hut, and pulled the hide curtain tight across the doorway. It was fiery hot, so hot it made their lungs ache.

"Climb up on the shelf," Pakkanen ordered, "and lie down."

The boys climbed up some logs to stretch out on the sod shelf where the earthen bricks were already almost too hot to touch. They were both dripping with perspiration.

"My eyeballs are searing," said Havelok. He started to raise his arm to shield his eyes, and then thought better of it. The air up there was too hot to move.

"We shall roast here like pigeons on a s-spit!" said Hugh Raven.

"Well—if you cannot stand it," said Pakkanen, "you can go any time. The boys of my country would laugh at you. It is nowhere near hot enough for a proper sauna." He added more wood to the crackling flames.

"I am like a greased pig," sputtered Havelok. "All lard and melting away in streams."

Pakkanen snorted. He poured water on the hot rocks that bordered the hearth. The water hissed and crackled. Steam rolled in waves over the two boys.

"Now!" said Pakkanen. He took out a handful of twigs, climbed the steps and began beating the boys with the wet leaves and twigs.

"Ow!" yelled Havelok. "Stop it!"

"Then beat yourselves," said Pakkanen. He handed them each a bundle of twigs.

The two boys sat on the edge of the sod bench and tried to beat themselves with the twigs. The blows were feeble, since they had no strength left from the heat. They watched Pakkanen vigorously whipping at his red and streaming body. Perhaps they could do it if they stood down below.

They climbed down and each of them beat the other until they were as fiery red as the Finn. They scrubbed themselves with handfuls of fine, dried roots and Gunnild's homemade soap.

"Into the river now!" shouted Pakkanen. He dove through the doorway. He raced down the beach to plunge into the stream.

The boys followed. They gasped at the shock of the cold water. Afterward it took every ounce of strength they had to put on their tunics. They lay in the stiff meadow grass, limp and exhausted, but filled to the brim with a feeling of well-being.

"I feel as clean and bright as a silver spoon," said Havelok, dreamily. He rolled over on his face. "Soon I shall have strength enough to fight a hundred dragons."

"I could eat one," said Hugh Raven. "I'm *s-starved!*"

"It is why the boys of my country are so strong," said Pakkanen, tossing kelp balls, keeping six of them in the air at once. "They can run a hundred miles behind a dog sled without tiring. Any two of them can run down a reindeer. They can ski or jump and throw huge logs or rocks, beyond any man's belief."

"I shall come every day to this sauna," said Havelok. He sat up and finished tying his shoes. "But first I have to sharpen Grim's ax."

Pakkanen grinned as he turned three somersaults in the air before his feet touched the ground once more.

While the sauna was being finished, Grim and his two older sons had gone fishing. They had netted and hooked a fine lot of fish. They took these in their nets to the town. They traded them there, with some silver money as well, for a cow and a calf, a butter churn, and flax thread ready for weaving.

William Wendut made wooden handles for the iron plowshare they had brought from Denmark. Gunnild kneaded flour with milk from the new cow and a little of the blessed water they had brought with them in a small flask. She baked a loaf as broad as a lamb's tail and laid it in the first plowed furrow.

Then William Wendut made bows and feathered arrows for the two boys. They got leave from Grim to go into the woods for any small game they could get.

"Do not go far," Grim warned them. "And be careful you do not shoot the Jarl's deer."

Havelok had been trained in archery. He taught Hugh Raven what he knew. It was poor hunting when they failed to bring back some meat for the pot, a squirrel, a fat hare, blackcock, and partridge.

They did not have to go too far for this small game. They were afraid to go deeper into the woods themselves. They did not say as much to each other, but both of them knew there were strange beasts and elfin maids and trolls in the Daneland woods. How much worse must the creatures be in these English forests!

How would you know what these creatures were? How would you understand them if they spoke? If you did not know what they were, what prayers could you use against them?

Whenever they heard a rustle in the woods the boys touched the bits of iron in the small sacks that hung around their necks for protection against witches and werewolves.

They had been almost a month in this place which was known roundabout by now as Grimsby. Pakkanen stayed with them saying it was overlate to take ship for Norway where the fiords were frozen. He would stay in England until spring. Perhaps he would go south to Lincoln, to sing for the Earl.

But there always seemed to be too much to do, a loft to build, a loom to set up, a sty to fence.

He had pounded out two crude broadswords of iron. He taught Havelok and Hugh Raven to defend themselves against his sword play in fine clashing battles.

"I cannot teach Havelok to read Latin," he said to Grim, "nor to write as a king's son should. He knows a little of these things now. It will have to do. He has had some training in war play, and he is afraid of nothing. If I can teach him to parry a spear thrust or a sword slash, it may stand him in better stead than Latin."

They found plenty of fish both to eat and to trade. Grim built a small storehouse, dug into the hill by a spring of sweet water. Here they put the barrels of salted fish for the winter. Here they stored the smoked meat that hung from the rafters of the hearth house until it was hard and black. They set out the milk bowls here for the cream to rise for the churning.

Havelok and Hugh Raven spent what time they could

coax from Grim hunting in the open uplands above the river, or in the fringes of the forest that came down to the sea. They clambered over the sea rocks and brought home shellfish, and eggs stolen from the nests in the cliffs.

Here Havelok would be lost in wonder over the perfect pattern of a starfish or the beauty of the pink-throated shells that sang in his ear. He would stand still, staring at a wedge of wild geese winging southward. "Where do they come from?" he asked Hugh Raven.

"Grim s-says they must winter underground. Caves maybe. They will fly north when the long nights are over and the s-snow begins to melt."

They came home smelling of seaweed and sweat. Pakkanen drove them out of the house to the sauna where he had built up a roaring fire. "Hot enough to roast a suckling pig!" complained Hugh Raven.

The leaves fell yellow and red and gold, crackling underfoot. Pakkanen set out traps, now that the fur had thickened on the pelts. He told the boys to run his trap-line and bring in what catch they could find.

They had no luck with their own hunting this day. But from Hugh Raven's belt there hung a small red fox and a yellowish ermine they had taken from the traps. Chewing the resin they had found on a bleeding pine, they came out of the trees to a broad sea-meadow, all brown now with the tall dead spikes of summer flowers rattling and whispering in the wind.

They walked down to the dune-sand. As they stood with the sea wind riffling their hair, a hawk dropped from where it had been waiting on. It stooped to a snipe mincing along the wet sand below the night's tide mark.

The strike had been swift and perfect. Both hawk and quarry were gone before the boys had caught their breath.

"A long-winged hawk!" cried Havelok. "A falcon, I think. Watch her! Mark where she goes."

They watched the bird fly straight and true to a high cliff above the water.

"Come on!" shouted Havelok.

"Where to?"

"We'll have to climb up the rock. It's late for nestlings. If the eyases are not too big, we can bring them home and train them to hunt for us."

"Only nobles can fly falcons," said Hugh Raven.

"True," answered Havelok. He put his bow and arrows on a flat rock. "Leave your pelts here. Hide them in the rocks. We had better take the sack with us."

Hugh Raven could never remember that climb when he thought back on it. All he could see were Havelok's feet and legs up ahead of him. All he could hear were Havelok's grunts and the water as it sloshed over the rocks a hundred feet below. His hands were cut and bleeding as he felt for hand holds. He dared not look down.

They found the nest of moss and dried grass on a high ledge. The mother bird had gone off. The fledglings were hopping and flitting from one side of the nest to the other, hissing and screaming as the boys' hands and arms came up over the edge of the flat ledge, and they each hooked an elbow over the rock.

Havelok braced himself by shoving his knee in a crack. With his free hand he reached out and caught the legs of the nearest eyas. The young bird bit him savagely. "Hold the sack open," he panted.

Havelok shoved the bird into the sack. His hand was bleeding from a deep gouge and he sucked it off before he reached for the second bird. The eyas jumped back across the nest with a scream of fury. Havelok pulled himself higher and caught the bird by the legs, grunting as the sharp curved beak slashed at his bent fingers.

This one too was popped in the bag. Hugh Raven tied the bag to his belt in back, so he could use both hands on the rock. All the way down they were fighting off the parent birds who were screaming and diving on them from above.

Once safely down, Havelok's eyes were shining. "What luck to get both of them! One for each of us."

Grim was not pleased when he saw what the two boys brought home with them. "We have no time to hunt meat for hawks," he growled. "We need the meat they will eat for ourselves."

"They will bring us meat, Grim," coaxed Havelok. "As soon as we get them trained they will bring us meat. I shall make them hoods for their heads and jesses for their feet. I will make a perch for them and lures to call them back to us."

"Learning to train a falcon," said Pakkanen, "is one way to learn to train one's self. No?"

"So it is with fishing," said Grim.

"Would you make a fisherman of Havelok?"

"He could do worse."

"That is true. Many of Christ's apostles were fishermen. But Birkabeyn's son could learn a lot from a falcon."

"Well, he must kill his own fresh meat for them, then," said Grim grudgingly.

Havelok was wild with delight. He would have dumped the birds out of the sack then and there, to show his prizes.

Pakkanen stayed his hand. "Take them to the sauna. Keep it dark and quiet. Do nothing in haste while they are at hand. Keep your voice quiet. Hold your anger. These are wild things, fierce and proud. What you do now for these birds will make or mar them for life."

Havelok lifted the sack from the floor and stilled the frantic struggles of the birds. He had lost his first wild excitement. In his face there was only concern.

"William Wendut, will you nail some sticks together for a perch? We'll need some cloth to cover it," said Pakkanen. He said to the boys, "You had better sit up with them tonight and feed them every few hours."

"Will they eat?"

"Not willingly. But when they open their mouths to scream at you, push the meat into their gorge with a small stick."

"Are there some woolen socks we can use to hood them?" asked Havelok.

"Yes," said Gunnild. "There are some old ones I was going to unravel for wool. Get Robert the Red to lend you his heavy skin gloves. You will need them."

"Where will we get meat for them?" asked Havelok as he and Hugh Raven set out for the sauna with Pakkanen. He carried the sack with the two birds. Hugh Raven had a perch and some jesses newly cut from old, soft leather with slits for thongs to hold the birds.

Pakkanen lifted the small leather sack he held. "I have cut up the hearts from the game you brought from the traps, and some other tender bits. They are in this sack."

"I have not trained a falcon before now," said Havelok uneasily. "I have hooded them and carried them and flown them. But training them sounds—well—not so easy as when I first thought of it."

Pakkanen's eyes twinkled as he glanced sideways at the boy and his sack. "It is not easy. A hawk is a keen judge of the people who work with her. Can you keep your voice and actions gentle, no matter how much she provokes you? Can you be patient no matter how slowly she learns? Any rough and angry treatment is resented. I have seen a hawk take delight in aggravating an impatient trainer. A falcon is a proud and haughty bird whom kindness alone will win."

"Will the Earl be angry if we fly falcons?" asked Hugh Raven. "He does not know that Havelok is king-born, but he would be s-sure that I am not."

"I do not think that anyone will carry the word to him. If they should, then you must say that you are apprentice falconers, flying the birds for Pakkanen of Finland."

"You have flown falcons before this," said Havelok.

"I have done many things." Pakkanen lifted the curtain of the sauna. "Both good and bad. The good things I have mostly forgotten, except for the whiteness of my mother's hands, the blueness of the lakes of Finland, and a brown falcon on my wrist."

"And the bad?" asked Havelok, setting down his bag with great gentleness.

Pakkanen laughed. "The bad will keep my dreams

troubled, my feet wandering, and my wits nimble, since I must sing for my supper."

He lit a candle and poured grease in a thick puddle on the high shelf. In the grease he set the candle and pushed the hot grease up around it.

"Let the birds out slowly, because the light will frighten them. Here are some small sticks to stroke them with, and to feed them."

Hugh Raven held an eyas while Havelok pulled a sock over its head and down around its shoulders. With his hands well-gloved he lifted it gently to the perch. The two birds were quiet, once the hoods were on. Their talons clutched the padded crossbar of the perch. Their gaping beaks poked out of holes in the socks.

Havelok put a piece of meat on a stick and offered it to one of them. As the meat touched her beak she screamed and plunged headlong off the perch, to the end of the leash fastened to the leather jesses around her legs. Hugh Raven lifted her gently back and this time Havelok managed to get the meat far enough down her throat so she was forced to swallow.

"She took it!" he cried. At the sound both birds bated off the perch, hissing and screaming and beating their wings.

Havelok was as startled as the eyases. "There now! There now!" he crooned, stroking their shoulders with the small stick.

Pakkanen slipped out through the hide curtain and returned to the hearth house.

"Well, what about this foolishness?" demanded Grim.

"It may not be so foolish," answered the Finn. "It takes great patience to gentle a hawk. The king's son will need patience before he is through, both for his hawk's training and for his own."

x

The Return of Horda

The male hawk that Hugh Raven trained was the more dependable of the two birds. Grim's son had a quiet way with him. His slow speech had a soothing tone to which his tercel responded.

Havelok demanded more of his brown and gray "Lady." He flew her at partridges and woodcook and hares, at herons and ducks. Even as a young hawk she would bind to heavy game and bring it down. But she was slower than the tercel coming in to the lures, the small bundles of feathers and fur the boys had made to swing at the end of a long thong. There were some days when she was sulky and indifferent to the food she was offered, or the tirings left for her to pick at.

Once she stayed away for two days, hiding from them. They called for hours. Havelok swung the lure until his arms were aching. He was wild with grief and worry. The third day she stooped to a blue heron and brought it down almost at Havelok's feet.

He was hard put to it not to scold her. Only the Finn's

warning kept him from punishing her by holding back her food.

Pakkanen stayed with them until the end of September. By Michaelmas he had trapped many hares, skinned and dried and softened the pelts.

Gunnild made a tunic of the skins, neatly sewn together. She edged it with gray squirrel fur. Pakkanen bought new shoes in the town with some of his furs. These were green, of fancy cut. He had green leather strippings to bind up his long hose, and a cap of green with a brown and gray barred hawk's feather.

Word had come that the Earl had brought his court north from Winchester to Lincoln, to collect his rent monies from the northern shires.

With his bone harp in a new sealskin case, and his staff in his hand, Pakkanen looked brave and gay as he set out for the court to sing himself into favor there. His leather shirt was open at the throat and the amulet of strangely woven metal tinged with green could be seen just below the hollow of his throat.

Levive had made him a roll of peppery ox sausage and a loaf of her crusty bread.

The whole family and Havelok walked with him along the road for a mile or more, loath to see him leave them. There was more than a touch of frost in the air and a film of frost rime in the hollows.

Hugh Raven had a hard time holding back his tears. Havelok's eyes were suspiciously bright as he trudged, his falcon on his wrist.

Pakkanen clapped his hands on their shoulders. "I will come back," he promised. "It has been good to be part of a family for this pleasant time." He held Dame Leve's hand for a long time, until they had all spoken their good will. Then he went striding off along the track through the heather as though it were any day, and he off to town.

"I'd have gone with him, if he had asked me," said Levive in a choking voice.

Grim looked at his younger daughter sternly. "'Tis a wanton thing to say, and uncalled for. He knows and we know that his roving ways leave no place in his life for a woman."

Gunnild put her arm around the younger girl. "We were lucky to have him this long. Come along, then. The butter needs churning and the cow needs milking."

"If the sky falls, the cow must be milked," answered Levive crossly.

Before All Saints' Day brought the end of the harvest Pakkanen returned. He came at night. It was so dark and the clouds so heavy with rain that moon and stars were hidden in the murk. He scratched on the house door and roused Grim from his first sleep.

Between the cracks in the loft floor Havelok could see them where they sat by the fire for a long time, talking in whispers. Havelok lay in the loft straw, with the scent of apples and dried herbs all about him, worried about what this night's meeting might mean. He felt a deep sadness when he saw Pakkanen rise from the floor beside the hearth, gather his cloak about him, and pick up his oaken staff. The Finn slipped away into the cold night without a greeting to any of the rest of them.

In the morning Grim called them about him. It was raining outside. As they watched through the open door the rain came slanting down like hissing spears, until the last of the red and gold leaves on the trees trembled and fell. The rain thrummed on the roof, and the house was full of the sound of the brook dashing and splashing over the rocks. Water fell like a gray curtain in front of the doorway, and bounced back from the paving stones of the garth, making a mist above the ground.

"Pakkanen was here in the night," said Grim, raising his voice above the sound of the waters. He held up his hand against their surprise. "Horda, Godard's man who swam to the death ship, has come to the court of Earl Godrich."

"If he has seen Pakkanen, he knows that I am here in England," said Havelok. "Is that it?"

Grim sighed. "I had hoped that no one would know of it until you were of size and stature to claim your rights."

Robert the Red slapped his thigh in anger. "Woe worth him! We should have killed him. We were fools to let him slip through our fingers."

"What is done, is done," answered Grim. "Pakkanen saw him come to the court with a pack-train of goods. He does not think that Horda saw him. Horda is a great man now with money and jewels, rich clothes and many servants. Earl Godrich has welcomed him. The two are hand and glove in all kinds of schemes. This need not concern us."

"Did he rob the death ship?" asked Havelok.

"Pakkanen feels sure that is the source of his wealth. His jewels are of ancient make and strange design. But Pakkanen says too that if Horda knows where Havelok is, he will try first to get money for his silence from us, and then more money from Godard for the telling."

"He promised he wouldn't tell," said Hugh Raven.

"That was before he had all these riches," scoffed Robert the Red. "He has just got his snout in the pail, this swine."

"A promise from Horda is a thin straw to lean on," said Grim.

"What will Pakkanen do?" asked Gunnild.

"He will return to the court. He has been there long enough to please the Earl and his ladies. There would be a hue and cry after him. He came to let us know about this, and to warn us to keep Havelok from the town until he sends us word that Horda is gone."

"I think we should go there and kill Horda," said Robert the Red, his mouth set and angry beneath the soft red down on his upper lip.

"And have wergild to pay for the deed, and forfeit all our lands here?" asked William Wendut.

"What does Pakkanen counsel?" asked Gunnild. She tucked her spindle beneath her arm as she twisted the thread in deft fingers.

"Horda is bound to know Pakkanen when they meet. But the Finn will tell him that we settled in Norway."

"What if Horda does not believe that?" asked William Wendut. He put down the wooden bowl he was carving. "Pakkanen was with you when you went to see Earl Godrich about the rents. The Earl knows well enough that we are here on this coast."

Grim shrugged. "We will cut a tree to bridge that stream when we come to it."

For a few days Havelok was kept at home. But when no further news reached them from Pakkanen, they began to think that Horda was gone, and no longer a threat to them.

About a week after the Finn had come to Grimsby in the night, Havelok and Hugh Raven took the hawks to fly them on the slopes above the duck ponds.

Havelok had slept poorly. He had been scolded the night before by Grim, for forgetting to bring in the wood to the hearth house, before leaving to fly his hawk with Hugh Raven.

He had not dared to answer Grim, but he had stood sullen and angry before him. His back was stiff, his fists clenched. He kept his eyes on his feet to hide the glitter of resentment.

"We all work here," Grim told him. "Even your hawks earn their food. It is a measure of a man's growth that he stands up to his responsibilities. You are responsible for the wood to burn in the hearth house."

Havelok wanted to shout at him that he and his hawk had brought in more food than anyone else except Grim himself. But as he had learned to curb his outbursts in front of his hawk, so he had learned to hold his tongue in anger. His night had been long and his sleep restless, after the scolding.

This morning he had chopped and brought in twice the daily load of wood, stacking it against the wall. When Gunnild thanked him, he did not answer.

He and Hugh Raven set off up the small stream that led to the uplands, carrying their hawks. Hugh Raven had gathered up two broken traps as they climbed the steep path.

Havelok stalked ahead, glum and silent. The first snow had fallen and was slippery on the rocks. There were showers of snow from every tree they brushed against. The cold bit at the flesh. Down the steep slopes the snow had rolled in little balls and the wind had carved out the centers of them. They looked like the fat little wreath cakes Gunnild made for Twelfth-night.

"Hold up, 'Lok. I have all this gear," panted Hugh Raven. "I can't keep up with your long legs."

Havelok didn't answer. He strode on at the same pace, one foot in front of the other. His hawk stirred on his wrist, moving her taloned claws restlessly. "Shoo! Shoo!" crooned Havelok.

Hugh Raven caught up with him. "Why are you s-so cross?"

"I am *not* cross."

"Well, you haven't s-said a pleasant word to anyone but Lady all day. Ever s-since Pakkanen left you have gone back to ordering us around. If 'twas he who kept you good humored–"

"I am perfectly good humored."

They had almost reached the first of the duck ponds.

"Want me to work around and send the ducks up, when Lady is waiting on?" asked Hugh Raven.

"I'll send them up myself," answered Havelok.

Hugh Raven turned his back and started up the slope to the upper ponds. He climbed in a zigzag, avoiding the outcrops of slick rock where the snow lay fast-melting in the sun.

Havelok looked after him, biting his lip. He started to call to him, glanced at his hawk, and held his tongue. He loosened the leather hood with his free hand and teeth. Lady's fierce golden-brown eyes blinked in the sunlight. She fluffed her feathers and warbled, reaching her wings high over her head. She stretched one leg out sideways and backwards.

"A-a-ah!" sighed Havelok. He loosed the leash that held the jesses. There was a tinkle from the small bells that William Wendut had made for the hawks.

Lady took off in a slanting line up and out. One wing was higher than the other, in perfect balance against the wind. Higher and higher she circled. Now she seemed no bigger than a wren. Now she was a tiny black speck against the deep blue of the sky.

Havelok had forgotten Hugh Raven and his own ill humor. He ran up the slope toward the duck pond shouting, "Howit! Howit!" A duck flew up and the black speck plummeted from the sky in a stoop so fast it was hard to follow.

There was good hunting that afternoon as boy and hawk worked together. Havelok praised Lady and stroked her gently with the stick he wore at his belt. He fed her choice bits from her kill. She preened her feathers, looking proud and pleased, until he hooded her and started home.

On the track where the forest met the sea-meadow, close behind a huge holly bush, a man was waiting. He sat astride a dun horse with wicker snowshoes bound to its hoofs.

Havelok shifted Lady to his right wrist, busy tying the

dead ducks to his belt. He was almost on the horseman before he saw him.

It was Horda.

The Norse man's helmet was painted blue, with wide horns set in gold. His dyed hair looked as coarse as rope hemp. His byrnie was massive with heavy links of metal that clashed and clanked as he turned. His silken tunic was spotted and soiled. About his neck hung ancient chains of gold and beads of amber. His hairy hands were weighted down with rings.

Havelok remembered his crafty, slit-eyed face in the firelight at Grim's house. He also remembered him in the bottom of the boat, with his battered face. He could see the scar of it on cheekbone and temple.

Horda drove his horse forward to block Havelok's path. "What is your name, boy?"

"I am Bjorn Grimsson," answered Havelok. He jerked his arm and the hawk on his wrist screamed and bated off with thrashing wings. "Easy, Lady. Easy," soothed Havelok, setting her again on his gloved wrist, stroking her with a crooked finger.

Horda laughed. "Good hunting, huh? Do they let fisherfolk fly falcons in England?"

"I am an apprenticed falconer, flying this falcon for my master."

Horda snorted. "And your master?"

Havelok dared not name Pakkanen to this man.

There was a shout behind him. "'Lok! Hey, 'Lok! Wait for me."

"Your brother does not call you Bjorn? Could 'Lok be short for Havelok?"

"Who are you to question my name?" asked Havelok angrily.

"You know well enough who I am, my lord." There was mockery in Horda's tone. "As a good Dane I am quick to recognize Birkabeyn's son."

"What do you want here?"

"Not so fast. Not so fast, king's son."

"If you want to talk with me it must be with my father at hand."

"Fair enough. I came here to talk with Grim, who is a fisherman and no father of yours."

Hugh Raven came up. Havelok thought with a grin that, if he had not known before, Horda must know now about Havelok, from Hugh Raven's face.

The early dusk had fallen. It was shrieking cold. Frost fire glimmered in the frozen hoofprints.

They followed the stream down to where Grim was working on his house in the last of the day's light.

Horda jumped down from his horse and handed the reins to Hugh Raven. "Rub her down," he ordered.

Hugh Raven tied the horse to a ring outside the door. He returned to stand with Havelok.

Grim climbed down the ladder and faced Horda. "Do you come in peace, Dane, or with shield-ring?" he asked.

"Peace, of course. I had heard that there were old friends of mine here-abouts. I came to greet them. Our last parting was a sudden one. No?"

Grim did not ask him into the house, but stood with him in the in-yard.

"It was the Earl who told me that you were here," said

Horda. "I have not told Godard that Birkabeyn's son is alive."

Grim remained silent.

"I came to you first."

"What for?" asked Grim. "I have only what you see here. It would soon be gone, and then you would go to Godard anyway."

"Not so," answered Horda. "Your friend Pakkanen has pointed out to me that this would be a foolish thing for me to do."

"Did he so?"

"Yes. Though why he should concern himself in my affairs is hard to see." Horda cracked his knuckles and smoothed the dirt-spotted sleeves of his silken tunic. He looked annoyed. "I was well pleased when the Earl told me that Grim Fisherman was here—here in England. It opened up a number of possibilities for me. You can see that?"

"I can see it."

"But this Finn, he tells me that there is a law in this land against the robbing of graves or of death ships, either one. To tell the truth I think these lawmakers mean to keep these rich treasures for themselves."

Grim said nothing to this.

"Pakkanen says if Godrich learns that I have money and jewelry and silken goods from this death ship, he will have me stripped and hung."

"I can see this," said Grim, a glint in his eye.

"Yes." Horda pulled at the long beard that flowed down on either side of his pocked chin. "Well, we are matched then. I cannot just now return to Denmark. A little matter of difference between me and Jarl Godard, seeing that I killed a man in the Thing-place, and was outlawed for it. It will blow over in time. But I choose to stay in England for a season."

Grim waited.

"Pakkanen has sworn that he will not tell about the death ship. If you swear this too, Grim—why then I can keep my promise about Birkabeyn's son." He grinned. His broken teeth looked wolflike behind the hedge of his beard.

"Good enough," agreed Grim. He placed his hand in Horda's hand. They both swore, Grim in God's name, and Horda in Odin's.

Then Horda mounted and turned his horse to ride away.

Havelok watched him go with heartfelt relief.

The boys took their hawks off to the small hawk house, a warm, snug place they had built. They fed their birds and talked to them. They hooded them and fastened them to the perches, leaving them in peace and quiet after the day on the downs.

They went off to build a fire in the sauna, to sweat and beat themselves warm and clean. By the time they came out there was a gale blowing, a wild storm of frozen rain. It took all the courage they had to run through it and plunge into the icy river.

Inside the hall the spears of sleet rattled against the stretched membrane of the window holes. The hearth fire was warm and bright.

"I cannot help feeling," said Robert the Red, "that we

should rid ourselves of this treacherous Dane. The sooner the better."

"We have, I think, less cause to fear Horda right now," answered Grim, "than he has to fear us. I doubt if Earl Godrich would believe his talk of a boy-king living with fisherfolk. But he would be quick to believe about the death ship. Right now Horda dares not go back to Denmark to carry the tale to Jarl Godard."

"Just the same," grumbled Robert the Red, "I will be glad when his sins catch up with him, this grave-robber."

xi

The Famine

Grim knew both the way of fish in the sea and the way of seed in the ground. With his sturdy boat and his sons to help, he caught many loads of fish, both in the sea and up the river. On land he grew good crops of flax and corn.

Levive had plaited great carrying baskets of reeds. These Grim filled with the fish he did not need to feed his family. He sold the fish to the farmer folk of the upland, and in the town of Lincoln. He returned with empty baskets and a purse full of pennies. Folk gladly bought his sea-food, knowing it fresh-caught.

In the town he bought meat and horn-shaped cakes and dried currants. He bought hemp to make the strong nets for his fishing. He brought home colored threads for weaving or metal for William Wendut to make into a pin to fasten a cloak, or shape into a plate for the church in the village.

By now Grimsby was a goodly steading with smooth walls of turf or rock, whitened with lime. Grim had built a long hall that stood broadside to the garth, with two hearths and built-in beds. The family lived at one end, and the beasts of the stable at the other. The pig and goat houses and the shearing pens were farther from the house.

Between the hearth house and the river were the acres of plowed ground, some fallow, some seeded. A fair mead-land lay along the brook.

The doors of the house were carved with twists and twinings of strange beasts and serpents and a fierce raven brooding over all the rest. Both inside and out there were fair carvings.

Gunnild said of William Wendut, "He cannot bear to see a smooth piece of wood without laying a chisel to it."

Twice in the years of Havelok's growing Pakkanen returned to Grimsby. Once he came with a donkey loaded down with sacks of shells from Ireland, shells that could be crushed to make a fine, purple dye. These were highly valued by weavers, and mightily pleased Gunnild and Levive.

He stayed long enough to help Havelok and Hugh Raven build a coracle, a small round boat of leather stretched over a frame of thin willow laths. In it the boys could fare up the Humber to fish in the shallows, or cross the wide river mouth to hunt in the northern uplands. The little boat stank of fish and was cranky in the tide currents, but the two boys loved it dearly.

Another time the Finn came back to nurse deep wounds. He lay for many days burning with fever, while Levive and Gunnild watched over him night and day. Levive brewed him cooling drafts from wood-herbs, and laid on the deep cuts soft cloths with healing salves.

Pakkanen told them nothing of the wounding. But

when he left he buckled on a sword of Grim's, and a short dagger. He grinned at the two boys watching him gird on the war gear.

"A little business of mine own to finish," he told them. He danced about them, flicking his sword until the light along the edge of it stabbed into their eyes. When he had shoved the sword back into its leather scabbard, his ice-blue eyes were sparkling with glee.

They had no way of knowing how this business went with him, for a year's time. Then one day a singer came to Grimsby with the sword. "The Finn said to tell you," he said, "that his serpent came forth from his scabbard and gorged himself with gore."

Grim's sons grew into stalwart men. His two daughters bloomed into beauty. They were known throughout the countryside as women of virtue, well-guarded, and skilled in household arts and leechcraft. There were few in the land roundabout who entered or left life without the helping hand of one of Grim's daughters.

The farmer's sons sent their fathers to ask Grim's consent to their son's wooing of one or the other. But Grim answered all of them that he would not wed his daughters away from home without their choosing. Since Levive and Gunnild had never found anyone to their liking, and chose to bide at home, busy and content, nothing came of it.

Some of their neighbors thought hardly of Grim in these matters. But it takes two to make a quarrel. Grim went his way taking no offense at what was said of him. It was hard to stay angry with a man so willing to lend his strong oxen for a day's plowing, or whose daughter brought her skill and soothing hands to ease a grandson into the world.

Havelok was something else.

He had lengthened out into a six foot six inch youth, strong and powerful. He was broad of shoulder and slim-hipped. His hands, big and gentle, were yet well-used to an ax, and calloused from the handling of nets and oars. His fair hair was wavy and fine, brushed back off a high forehead. His blue eyes, with a rim of darker blue around the iris, were set wide in a windburnt face. There was a dash of color on his cheekbones. He had a hard jaw and jutting chin, softened with a dimpled place beneath his lip. He kept the fine, fair down of his upper lip and cheeks shaved close with a cowrie shell, well-sharpened.

Havelok had come to realize that while he hunted and hawked, Grim was working hard to get him food. The thought came to him that he was no longer a child. He was full-grown and eating more than two of his foster brothers.

"I shall go now and earn my keep," he told Grim. "Work is no shame. The shame is that I have not seen it was needful. I too can carry baskets and sell fish."

The next day at sun-up he took the heavy baskets on his shoulders. By himself he lifted as much as Grim and his three sons could carry. He laid the silvery fish cool and beautiful in the baskets. He delighted the housewives with his courtesy and banter. He sold all the fish and brought home every penny, keeping not even so much as a farthing.

All these years there had been plenty of food. There was wheaten porridge and fresh fish cooked on a shovel in the ashes, or a rich lentil soup with Levive's sweet bread. There were berries and greens in season, and fruit from the wind-bitten trees on the hill. Small game brought in by bow and trap and hawk gave them food to eat and clothes to wear and warmth to cover them through the winter's cold.

In these days Grim thought much about the matter of his foster son, seeing that Havelok was now full-grown. He watched his light, quick movements and saw that he could wield a sword as well as an ax. He knew that Havelok could bend a bow of many pounds' pull, and send a spear high in the air and catch the quivering shaft as it hurtled down upon him.

Havelok was ready, Grim was thinking, to go back to the country of his birth, and fight for his kingdom. But how that was to come about, the old fisherman did not know. A man could not fight for a kingdom by himself. It would need more than three foster brothers, strong and loyal as they were, to win him back a throne.

When Havelok was nineteen winters old there came a year of great dearth in England. The whole east coast lay under a famine. Men could not remember so bitter a winter in all the times they knew.

The merchants and men of the court in Lincoln bought up all the stored food in the hamlets. They ranged far afield to buy salted meat, and sent as far away as York for grain and cheese.

The rain held back for a whole season. The cold was cruel but there was little water in the ground. Great blocks of trees died in the wooded places. The wind blew wild and was as sharp as a honed knife. The earth was too hard and fast with black frost for the strongest plowshare shod with iron to break through.

The men of the fields shivered under the heaviest furs, and the doorposts and rafters cracked and split in the bitter cold. The fires on the hearths seemed to give but little heat and the smoke-reek hung blue and choking beneath the smoke holes.

A pale sun shone through a film of mist that swirled and eddied along the low places, until all the land seemed ghostlike and under some dread spell. Men talked of strange things seen in the woods. Women were afraid to be out-of-doors after sunset.

The corn came up spindly and yellow and set few heads on the stalk. The turf on the roof which each year had been a carpet of grass and flowers was hard dirt. The dry dust sifted down between the cracks and lay like a veil over all that was in the house.

Grim and his sons and Havelok sailed far to the north and to the south on the sea-road. But the fish had left the coast. The boat seldom brought back even enough to feed the family.

Dame Leve stole secretly into the woods to smear honey on an ancient oak. When the quick dry storms brought lightning crackling about the gables, she laid an acorn in the window. The priests prayed for rain and for patience with men who killed their horses to offer on the old and secret altars in the woods.

When hunger gnawed at him, Havelok touched the little silver cross that hung on a thong about his neck. He sent up many an earnest prayer for food to save the foster family who had given him so generously of all they had.

Grim did not know how he could feed his family. They were down to eating the seed corn in the storehouse, and grubbing for roots in the forest. Levive made a bread of fir bark and rye and it was bitter fare. She pounded the few acorns and beechnuts she could find into a meal, leaching out the bitterness with hot water, but there was no meat to add strength and flavor.

It was at this time that an old woman came to Grimsby asking for food. Her hair was snow white, her skin brown and wrinkled. Her bare feet were red with cold. She was as bony as an unfeathered bird fallen from a nest, but her eyes were honey-colored and clear as birdsong.

"For the love of God and His Son, will you give me a bite to eat in my hunger?"

Grim could not turn her off, she seemed so old and to be pitied. "We have little enough for eight," he told her, "but it can always stretch to cover one more."

She called down a blessing on his head and put out a skinny hand for the dark bread Gunnild brought her.

When Havelok came in and saw her there, dipping her dry bread in a thin root gravy to soften it, he remembered her. "You are the woman of the woods who told me many years ago that I had two stars in my hand," he said, smiling down at her. "God's greeting to you, mother."

She looked up at him, her amber eyes intent, her eyelids blue-veined and thin as flakes. She caught at the big hand that hung down by her face. She peered into the horny palm of it. She traced the outline of a rune in the air. "Aye. I had forgotten. Two stars and a journey joining them."

"When will we take this journey?" Havelok asked, more to please her than for any other reason.

"Soon. Sooner than you think."

In the morning, with no word to anyone, she was gone.

Grim lived with fear now because of Havelok, who was so big and strong and could eat more food than two. He called him over to where he was working at his nets.

Havelok stood before his foster father. He towered over the old fisherman who was age-bent now with the long years of fighting the sea and the furrow. "What can I do for you, Grim?"

Grim put his hands on his knees where the net was spread. "My son, I think we shall soon perish of hunger, for our stores are long since gone. The fish have left the coast and the famine lasts. For me and Leve it matters little. We have lived our lives. But it is wiser for you to leave us now, while there is yet time, and seek work to do and food to eat. They say that Earl Godrich has come to Lincoln. There must be men there who would hire a stalwart lad willing to earn his bread."

Havelok looked down at the tunic that hung about his bulky frame in rags and tatters. He laughed. "I doubt if anyone would hire such a scarecrow."

"Alas that you should be so nearly naked!" cried Grim. "I will make you a coat of my old sail, to keep out the cold."

Grim made the coat and shaped it to Havelok's broad shoulders. Havelok thanked him and put it on.

Grim gave his foster son the jeweled pin and ring that had lain under the hearth in Denmark. "These are yours, king's son. They will bring you food if you are starving.

Otherwise use them as you see fit. They were on your hand and cloak when I took you home from Godard's hall."

Years before this Havelok and Hugh Raven had become blood brothers. They cut a length of sod and pulled it up into an arch, with the ends still bedded in the earth. With Havelok's sharp knife they cut their wrists and mingled their blood and dripped it on the arch. Then each crawled beneath the sod, though it was a tight fit for Havelok, and clasped hands afterwards. They swore fealty, the one to the other, until death. Both promised to avenge any wrong done to either one.

Grim and all his family walked with Havelok a long way, as they had done with Pakkanen. The women wept when he left them, but he laughed and jested with them until they laughed through their tears.

Hugh Raven walked another mile or so beyond the others. Neither Hugh Raven nor Havelok was ashamed of his tears as they parted.

With no other kind of dress than the old sail coat, and barefoot, Havelok walked the long way south to Lincoln.

xii

Goldborough

Havelok had no friends in Lincoln. He did not know where to turn for food or housing. For two days he went hungry, since the small bit of food Grim could give him was eaten on the journey. He felt lonely and way-lost.

The third day he went up toward the market place. He heard someone calling. "Bearing men! Porters! This way!"

In a wave-surge all the waiting folk sprang forward. With them was a tall man in a stiff white coat. Havelok shoved aside the others and strode to where the Earl's cook was buying meat and fish at the market by the bridge.

Before anyone could stop him he had shouldered the heavy basket and climbed the hill to the castle kitchen. For pay he got a farthing cake, which disappeared in one gulp.

The next day he watched for the cook. When he heard the call for bearing men, he knocked down sixteen strong lads who stood in his way. He ran with his fish basket and began snatching up the fish. The load he lifted was as much as a whole cartload. He spared neither his toes nor his heels until he came to the castle kitchen. The men who took the burden from his shoulders staggered under the weight of it. They marveled that any one man could have carried this heavy load up the hill from the bridge.

The cook looked at Havelok and the big basket of fish he had brought. He thought to himself, this is the strongest, stoutest bearing man I have yet seen. Aloud he asked, "Will you work for me, as kitchen scullion? I will feed you for your service."

It did not matter to Havelok to be called a scullion. "I would thank God for such hire," he said cheerfully. "If you will give me enough to eat, sir, I will build up your fires, sharpen and crack the sticks for eel skinning, and wash the dishes."

The cook was well pleased. "That is all I ask. Sit down and eat your fill.

Right gladly Havelok sat at the kitchen table. He ate until he had eaten enough for three. Afterwards he went to the well for a drink. Beside the well was a great empty tub with two rope handles. Havelok filled the tub and carried it alone to the kitchen, though it had needed a man at either handle before now.

Havelok would let no other porter fetch water or bring meat from the bridge. He brought in all the slabs of turf for the fires, and drew all the water that was needed from the well.

He was always merry and ready with laughter at another man's jest. When he was tired or low in spirits, he shut his feelings away. Those at the castle knew him only as a cheerful lad who liked to sport with the children of the kitchen folk.

Even beyond the castle men spoke of this scullion, of how strong he was, but gentle and friendly, and of how he went about his work clad only in a stiff and wretched coat of sailcloth.

The cook was sorry for Havelok. He bought him new clothes and stockings with leather strips to hold them, and leather shoes. Havelok was well pleased with these gifts. He put them on. When he was clothed in decent clothes no one was fairer.

The cook said of him, "Surely no one else in the kingdom seems more fit to be a king."

Havelok laughed at him. He went in to the kitchen to turn about and show the kitchen maids his new finery, for all the world like a small boy showing off his first leather shoes.

At the Lincoln games, that year and the next, when the Earl's men were gathered together, Havelok stood like a ship's mast, shoulders taller than the rest. At the wrestling games he overthrew all who came against him.

The second spring that Havelok was away from Grimsby, Earl Godrich sent for his barons and earls and men of consequence in England to come to Lincoln for a Parliament, for council and judgment. Various strong men and champions came too, to try their prowess in games and sports.

The farming folk, shepherds with their crooks, stable-boys with their goads, just as they had come from the plow or the sheepfold, gathered to watch and cheer on their favorites.

Several of the young men began to try their strength at stone putting. They chose a heavy stone, as weighty as a heifer. He was counted a stalwart man who could lift this stone to his knee. A champion would be the one who could heave it an inch beyond another's throw.

Havelok looked on. He had never seen men at this game before. It looked none too hard to him.

When he and his master had watched the men push and heave at the stone for awhile, the cook said, "Why not see what you can do with the stone, Havelok?"

Havelok was afraid he might shame the cook who had been so kind to him, but he strode forward and stood over the huge black rock. He could see for himself that this was a stone of strength, a stone strange to these parts and of great size.

Then he stooped and put his long arms around the angles of it. The muscles of his arms and legs stood out like the oak knobs where old limbs had fallen away. The cords of his neck sheeted down to his shoulder in a solid block. He lifted the big stone, straightened as he swung it a little, humming as he swayed. Then he heaved it in front of him with a whistling grunt, and pitched headlong after it.

From where he had first lifted it to where it thudded into the meadow, plowing a brown scar in the grass, was a distance of twelve feet or more. Never in any man's time who stood there had there been such a stone-throw as this.

A great groan went up from the men standing by to watch. One man pressed forward to measure the distance with long strides and the crowd counted his paces out loud.

Havelok dried his wet hands on a grass tuft and pushed

himself to his feet. He was laughing as he joined Bertram the cook, who was shaking his head at this marvel.

Men stood there after he was gone, with their mouths agape, as they stared at where the stone lay bedded in the greensward. A man drove a stake in where Havelok had stood because, he said, no one would believe it who had not seen it.

The champions who saw it shouldered each other and laughed. "We stay here over long," they said, and would strive no more.

Now the story of this feat could not be stayed. All through England went the tale of how this kitchen knave, this scullion, had put the black stone. Knights and champions told about it in castle and hall. Shepherds and swineherds and horse drovers talked of it on the hills and in the stables and mews of the towns. The distance of the stone putting grew with the stories that were told of it. All Lincolnshire and as far south as London they talked of this scullion, this porter and dishwasher, of how he was strong and fair and courteous as well.

Then Earl Godrich, hearing this talk, thought to himself, why not? Through this knave shall I and my son have England. On the Holy Book did King Athelwold make me swear that I would give his daughter to the tallest, fairest man in all England. From the tales they tell of this scullion, surely he is just the man. Now—though I search from end to end of England—where could I find another so tall and fair, so strong as this dishwasher? This is the husband that Goldborough shall have."

He scrubbed his hands together in glee as he thought of

it. He believed Havelok to be a churl's son, when he planned this wicked treason.

He sent men to Dover on the east coast, to bring the Princess to Lincoln.

A group of five men rode, with extra horses, to the tower on the coast where the Princess had long been imprisoned. It was late at night when they reached the tower.

One of the men dismounted and beat on the door, with the handle of his sword. The dark door creaked open. In the faint light of a horn lantern, the man who had knocked went inside. Those who waited could hear him climb the stairs.

It was a foul night. The waves beat on the shore cliffs with a rush and a hissing over the pebbles on the beach. Mist swirled about the tower and above the pools of tide water left behind in the rocks. Seabirds flew by in forlorn loneliness, mewing and creaking like lost souls.

"A beastly place," said one of the riders. "Who is it we have come to get?"

"Hush! It's like to be treason to even speak of this night's work. The girl in there can stretch all of our necks. It is best that you and I do not know too much."

"Is it she, then?"

"Aye," another muttered. "She who should be Queen of England by the rights of it. They say she is bonny."

"Don't be a fool," growled another. "If that gets to the ears of Earl Godrich, you're like to lose both of yours."

They were silent after that. There was only the sound of water and the ring of a horse's hoof on the hard rock of the tower garth.

Later the door opened and four figures came out, well-wrapped in cloaks. Another man held up a torch to light their way across the puddles in the rough stones.

"God's grace to you, gentlemen," said a breathless voice. "I grieve that you have come so far in such bitter weather."

No one answered and the voice did not speak again.

It was many nights later when they led the Princess to the room where Earl Godrich sat fingering a wine goblet, staring moodily into the empty ruby heart of it.

Goldborough bore herself proudly, in spite of her muddy clothes and her fine gold hair all disordered by the days of riding. She stood in the doorway, tall and quiet. The draft plucked at her long cloak. The candles guttered and sputtered. She heard the door close quietly behind her.

Earl Godrich looked at her, his black eyes squinting to see beyond the candlelight. "Sit down," he ordered.

She stood a moment longer, and then came slowly forward. She sat down on the end of the bench opposite him.

"Have you eaten?" he asked.

"No."

Food was brought. She ate daintily and deliberately.

When the servant had left the room, Goldborough looked up at the Earl sitting in the high seat in the king's hall. "Why have you sent for me after all these months?"

Earl Godrich stirred. There was a crafty look in his black and slanting eyes. "Because I have decided you are old enough for marriage."

If she started at this, she hid it beneath a quiet lowering of her hands to her lap. Her sea-blue eyes were fastened on his face.

Earl Godrich sat back in his high chair. He lifted one hand to stroke his silky black moustache.

Goldborough waited. She looked serene and sure of herself, but her hands were clasped so tightly together in her lap her knuckles were white.

"I promised Athelwold I would marry you to the fairest, strongest man in England." The Earl pursed his lips and drew them back over his teeth in a grin. "I have found him."

There was a long silence. "Who is he?" she asked at last. In spite of herself her voice was scarcely above a whisper.

His sickly crooked smile curved his thin lips but left his eyes as cold as a snake's eyes. "His name is Havelok. He is fair and strong. He will fulfill my promise to your father."

There was fear in her face now. "Of what mark is he?"

The Earl laughed. There was an evil look of triumph in his face. He said the words slowly, savoring their impact. "He is a Dane. He is the son of Grim, a fisherman—and a scullery knave."

She sprang to her feet, her face blazing with shame and fury. "I will marry no one who is baseborn!" she cried. "My father was King of England. I am his heir. I will not marry a kitchen churl. I will marry none save a king or a king's son."

Godrich rose and leaned across the table, as angry as she was. "Have done with this whining—"

She broke in. "What will you take that will buy my way out of this?"

He laughed and pursed his lips. "You have nothing. Even what you wear on your back I have given you."

"With monies from my lands," she pointed out, angrily. "I will deed you a fair number of lands and castles. . . ."

"They are mine now. All England is mine."

"I have friends," she said in desperation. "They will raise money and help me."

"If you so much as call on one of them," he told her, his voice savage, "I will put you in a nunnery. All your lands and goods will be forfeit to me."

"I will not enter a cloister and let England be ruled by you."

He leaned across the table and struck her with the flat of his hand. "You will wed this cook's knave tomorrow, or you go back to your tower and starve."

She turned away from him, her hand pressed on her reddened cheek. She was shaking from head to foot, but too proud to weep. He clapped his hands, and a woman came and led her away.

When she reached her room Goldborough threw herself in the arms of Hild who was waiting for her there.

"Oh, Hild!" she cried, weeping, weeping.

Hild held Goldborough's face tight against her. She patted her shoulder. After a bit she slid the damp hood back and unbuckled the heavy cloak. "See, now. Here, slide your dress off and slip into this. Sit by the fire and let me brush your hair."

Goldborough took off her damp and muddy dress. She let Hild drop the soft woolen night-sheath over her head. Hild brought her water and washed her face and hands and feet.

"Always and always have you waited on me with kindness, Hild," murmured the Princess. "I have not had much kindness, outside of you and Solvi."

"As long as we two can serve you, Lady, you will have kindness," answered Hild.

"Who knows how long that will be!" The Princess began to weep again. "He will marry me to a baseborn knave. Who knows where I will be?"

Hild went on brushing the long fair hair with steady strokes, keeping her voice low. "Listen, Princess. There is a woman who has come here, so old she looks ready to blow away. She asked me if she could see you. She said she had something to say about your marriage."

"Who is she? How did she know I was to be wed? I did not know myself."

"I do not know, Lady. But she is a woman of power, she is a foreseer."

"Where is she?"

"She is sleeping in the loft over the stable. She will be gone in the morning."

"Can you bring her here?"

Hild looked frightened.

"Bring her by the porches and through the hall," coaxed the Princess. "There is no one there at this hour. I am a fool to listen to anyone, but my mind is in a torment."

A half-hour later there was a scratching at the door. The Princess unbolted it. On the threshold was the oldest woman she had ever seen.

The old crone was withered and shrunk upon herself, so skinny her bones were not more than a skeleton. And yet there was in her face a kind of beauty that age pulls tighter about the bone. Her eyes were honey-dark beneath arched eyebrows as white as snow. Her nut-brown mantle and hood were lined with cat fur as tawny as her eyes. From her girdle hung a small bulging bag. On her feet were well-worn leather shoes with tin buttons.

"God's greeting to you, Princess," whispered the old woman, but she traced a rune in the air as she spoke. She slid inside the door and pulled it to behind her. She hobbled to the table and picked up the candle, holding it high so she could peer into the face of the Princess. As she pushed back her hood, her eyes gleamed in the candlelight like a badger's.

"Why did you come here, Mother?" asked Goldborough, half afraid the old woman might be witless.

"Because I must see if you would do for him."

"For whom?"

"The man you are to marry."

"This kitchen knave!"

"Ho! He is no kitchen knave. He is no fisherman. He is a king's son, with two stars in his hand."

"He is baseborn!"

The old woman let out a cackle of laughter. "No more baseborn than you, Lady. Marry him and he will crown you queen. Refuse, and you die." She hobbled to the door and turned back to Goldborough. Her clawlike fingers were feeling for the bolt. "It is as simple as that, Princess. You hold his life and yours in your own hands."

Goldborough reached to pull a ring from her finger to pay the old woman for her coming, but the door closed soundlessly before she could move.

In the morning Earl Godrich sent for Havelok. When

Havelok stood before him, the Earl was taken aback by his size. Nor had he expected a man of courtesy and courtliness. He hesitated as he saw Havelok's ease of manner.

"How can I serve you, my lord?" asked Havelok.

"Would you marry, churl?"

Havelok laughed. "Not I." He ran his hand down the back of his head. "What would I do with a wife? Where could I take a woman? I have no house or any land. What could we eat? Even my clothes are not my own, but belong to Bertram, the cook. All I own is an old white coat made from a fishing sail."

The words angered Godrich. The Earl started up and struck Havelok a blow on the ear. He was further angered when the knave stood and smiled at him.

"You will take the woman I give you to wive," the Earl gritted, "or else I will hang or blind you."

Then Havelok shrugged and agreed to it.

Goldborough too, though the very thought of it was as bitter as gall, dared not hinder the marriage. Through the long night she had put herself in God's hands.

The men and women who were serfs under Godrich had prepared the hall. Godrich had not ordered this done. They did this for the love of the gentle Princess, and to make her wedding a little more seemly. They spread fresh, sweet-smelling rushes on the floor, and laid a crimson cloth on the table by the high seat. They decked the bride-seat with the leaves and flowers of fruiting trees. They put new torches in the holders on the walls, and fair, honey-wax candles in silver holders.

The wedding was held before all the court. If there was

any murmuring, it died before the ugly look in the face of Earl Godrich.

Havelok came into the hall first, bearing in his hand two fair, blue ribbons. He looked around at all the company and saw not one kind or friendly face.

Then Goldborough entered. Havelok thought it was as though the sun had come through dark clouds to light a goodly field of ripened grain. Her hair was spread out in shining golden waves over her shoulders. It was like a mantle reaching to her slender waist.

Her dress was of blue stuff, soft and cunningly cut, with embroidery in gold and silver thread around the neck and sleeves. Her belt was set with agates, light and dark blue both, and ranging from her neck was a cross of rock crystal bound in gold.

Her face was pale and set, beneath a forehead as white as a privet flower. Her blue eyes had circles under them, for she had spent a sleepless night on her knees in prayer.

She sat on the bride-bench, tall and still, and there were no maids to sit beside her. Across from her stood Havelok, with no groom's men to stand with him.

Earl Godrich thought to shame Goldborough when he asked, "Is there a dower this maiden brings to her wedding?"

"Yes," answered Goldborough firmly. "Hild, my serving woman, and Solvi, my father's man, will bring my dower."

Hild entered holding one end of a small, heavy chest, while Solvi held the other. The chest was old and battered. The painted designs of leaping deer and birds were dimmed and scratched.

"My father, Athelwold of Britain, King in the sight of

God, gave me this dower for my marriage portion," Goldborough's voice rang out, daring Godrich to take her dower from her in the face of all this court.

On top of the chest there lay a golden crown, a slender circlet of gold, worked and woven. In the front of it was set a blue jewel that caught the light of the candles and shattered into rainbow colors.

Earl Godrich bit his lip. His eyes glittered with anger. He had not thought at any time to look into this battered

chest. Where had it been? No telling what it held. Now he was filled with regrets at his hasty action of marrying Goldborough to anyone.

The sight of the crown was a shock as well, until he remembered that in many lands all who were maidens wore a crown on their wedding day.

When Goldborough turned to Havelok, he smiled at her. Caught by surprise, she smiled back at him. Hild stepped forward and placed the golden circlet on Goldborough's shining hair. The jewel in the crown and the eyes below it flashed with the same blue-green sea color.

Havelok stepped forward and tied the blue ribbons to his belt and to hers.

The marriage service was said by the Archbishop of York. Havelok tied the ribbons in a lover's knot, when the words were said, and bent to kiss his bride.

The Princess drew back haughtily for just a moment, her blue eyes searching his. There was in her ears a cackle of laughter and an old voice saying, "No more baseborn than you, Lady." But it was not this that made her change her mind. It was the look in Havelok's eyes. He looked fearless and kind, strong and sound of body, gentle and generous.

She raised her face and he kissed her on the mouth.

Solvi and Hild lifted the heavy dower box and carried it away. They had promised Goldborough they would take it with them and guard it until such time as she sent for it. They had told everyone that they were freed of service now, and planned to be wed and live in Wales.

Havelok and Goldborough shared the same goblet of

mead, made with honey and wine. Afterward she stood with him to greet the court.

Then when Hild brought her a long, dark cloak and a bundle of clothes, she and Havelok left Godrich's hall. It wanted but an hour of high noon.

Now that the wedding was done, Havelok did not know what to do or where to go. It was plain to see that Godrich hated them, and already regretted what he had done. Havelok knew full well that shame would come to Goldborough in that she had married a kitchen knave.

As they stepped into the garth they met Bertram, the cook. In his hand Bertram held a short sword of good workmanship. It had a double blade, well-honed, and there were ancient runes carved on the blade of it.

"You may have need of this before the day is past, Havelok, to guard your lady and ours. There is a life-stone sunk in the hilt which will surely cure your wounds. The runes upon the blade have a song they sing,

For him who gets it
A ring is in the guard.
Courage is in the middle,
Terror is in the point,
A blood-dyed serpent
Lies along the edge."

Havelok was glad to have such a stout sword at his side. He thanked Bertram for this goodly gift. "I shall call this sword 'Thorn of the Shields.' I shall long remember the giver."

Havelok decided that he and his wife would flee to

Grim and his family, since there they could best hope for food and a roof over their heads.

They went on foot, since they knew no help for it. They held to the long way north until they came to Grimsby.

xiii

Grimsby

All the long way as they walked Havelok showed Goldborough every courtesy and kindness. He seldom touched her, except to lift her gently across the streams and muddy places. He walked close beside her in the dark woods. He called out greetings as they passed the men swinging scythes or spreading the new-cut, flowery hay to dry in the sun. The scent of the fresh hay was sharp and sweet. The Princess was to remember it all the days of her life with joy.

Now and then, along the way, Havelok would point out to her the places he had spent his boyhood. He told her of that first long walk to Lincoln and the sweet berry jam after the weeks of dried fish and hard bread on the voyage. He spoke to her of Pakkanen and Hugh Raven and the hawks. He talked of Dame Leve and Grim and his foster sisters.

The fields were hot under the sun, but after the sun went down the forest seemed full of gloom, and fearsome.

Goldborough came to know him a little, this big blond

man with his quiet ways and his easy, swinging stride. He seemed to her to be a courteous man, and certainly a comely one. But she hardened her heart against him, thinking him baseborn and not fit to wed a princess.

They walked until dark. Ahead of them the northern lights let down curtains of crimson light, trembling and pulsing, changing to an eerie green, fading away in thin, white clouds.

The stars and the moon were out in a dark sky, when they came down from the upland-wild to the cluster of buildings that was Grimsby. They could hear the water of the brook rushing over the stones. The river glinted below, all silver and moon-swept.

At Havelok's clear call Hugh Raven came leaping from the stable, shouting his welcome. The hall door was flung wide.

Sorrow met Havelok here. He learned that Grim had died, and also Dame Leve in the hard time of the famine. He remembered the days of Dame Leve's love and kindness, of her understanding and patience with a boy's careless ways. He thought of Grim and his sharing of all that he had with his foster son, and of how he had left his home and the land of his people.

But their five children were at Grimsby. They were all full of joy when they saw Havelok and his bride. They welcomed the weary travelers. "Now that the days of the famine are gone, we have goods and horses, nets and boats. Our crops have been good, and we have sheep and swine. Our father charged us to hold these things for you. All that we have is yours.

Hugh Raven, stuttering and stumbling, could not find

words to speak, but his merry eyes told Havelok he was overjoyed to see him once again.

William Wendut said, "You shall be our lord and we will serve you. Our sisters will wait on your lady, and make her bed and yours."

Levive and Gunnild built up the fires. When they had good cooking coals, they prepared meat and spared neither goose nor hen nor duck. There were thin slices of bear ham, and water cress to eat, with Levive's fine-grained bread, and soft cheese and honey cakes. For drink they had a morat of honey and mulberry juice.

Goldborough thanked them for all their good food. "It has been a wedding feast of plenty," she said in her golden voice, "all spiced as it has been with loving kindness."

They could see that Goldborough was weary, as she sat upon the bed that Gunnild and Levive had spread for her with the softest furs and the finest of all Levive's weaving. They helped her in all ways, and left her there with the crown shining on her outspread, golden hair, and her blue eyes drowned in tears.

The Princess was sad at heart, for all unfittingly had she been wed, she who was a princess who should be queen of all this land.

In the night she wakened. All about her there was a light, fair and bright like a white flame. It filled the room. She could see that it came from the mouth of Havelok, who slept beside her.

He is dead, she thought, or else most nobly born.

Then she saw on his shoulder the red cross that glowed in the light. "Surely it is a king-mark," she whispered.

Gunnild came to the bed to soothe her, saying, "Lady, is there anything I can do to serve you?"

"The light!" said Goldborough in a strained voice. She caught Gunnild's hand in both of hers. "What makes the light?"

Gunnild laughed joyously. "Let be your sorrow, Lady. He who has wedded you is a king's son. He is Denmark's right-born king. Queen of Denmark will you be, when he has won back his crown."

Goldborough was too happy to hide her joy. She stooped and kissed Havelok as he slept.

He wakened and started up from his sleep. "Lady, I have dreamed a strange and powerful dream. I dreamt I was in Denmark on a hill so high I could look out on all the world. As I stood there my arms grew long enough to reach around all of Denmark. All the things in that land cleaved to me. The keys of strong castles fell at my feet. All the people kneeled before me. And again I dreamed that I sailed over the salt sea to England. This land, too, I closed in my fist, and–Goldborough–I gave it to you."

"May Christ grant that this dream be fulfilled and gladden our hearts," said Goldborough. "I believe now that you will wear England's crown as well, and be King of Denmark, too. But go at once. Do not delay. Ask Grim's sons to go with you to Denmark, for they are loyal to you, and love you dearly."

With the first light of day, Havelok rose and went, before he did any other thing, to the church, to kneel and call on Christ and the Cross. He left his arms in the cloister-way and went in to pray. He gave thanks for the maiden he had married, and for her deliverance and his

own from the treachery of Earl Godrich. He called on God and Christ for help in winning back his own kingdom for himself, and her kingdom for his princess.

"O Thou, Who dost rule the wind and water, the wood and wold," he prayed, "of Thy mercy have pity on me, Lord. Let me and mine pass safely across the sea and bring me to that land of mine which Godard rules."

He laid his offering on the altar and returned home.

For a morning-gift Havelok brought to Goldborough the ring that had lain under the hearthstone in Denmark. It was wrought of twisted gold, deep-set with a blue stone that held in its heart a spark of ruby red. He slid it on Goldborough's slender finger, and kissed the hand that wore it.

Then all of the house of Grim brought bride-gifts to the lovely princess whose face was rosy with pleasure.

Levive brought her a red cow and her heifer calf, saying, "I will keep them until you can build a byre for them. The cheese and butter I will make and sell for you."

Gunnild laid in Goldborough's lap a dozen linen sheets, each embroidered with a crown in gold thread. "I have been making them for two years for Havelok's bride."

Goldborough praised the work. Truly, she thought, she had never seen such fair, fine linen weaving.

Robert the Red brought a belt with a silver key ring, and William Wendut a flame-grained bowl of cherry wood, satin-smooth, with acorns and oak leaves carved on the brim of it. Hugh Raven laid in her lap a fragrant rosary of beads made of wild rose petals, dried and rolled, with a cross of blue enamel that had been his mother's.

With the gifts all about her, Goldborough laughed and cried with her joy in them.

Afterwards Havelok called to him his three foster brothers. He told them what he meant to do. "Now that I am come of age, and am able to wield war-weapons, I must make my way to Denmark. I pray you, foster brothers, come with me. I will make all of you rich men if we win through this venture."

They did not hesitate, even for a breath. "We will come," said Robert the Red, and William Wendut echoed him. Hugh Raven laughed aloud. "And I—well, I —I would follow you to where the s-sea drops off and s-strange beasts lurk in the mists and depths at the end of the world."

Havelok's heart was singing, as he thanked them.

It was on this day that Solvi and Hild came to Grimsby. They told Goldborough they had left the chest in Lincoln, with the priest who had married them. He would hold it until Goldborough sent for it. They had been afraid to carry it with them, when they learned that Earl Godrich had sent men after them.

They were free now. The links of gold Athelwold had left them would buy them land and thralls of their own. But they said they would wait at Grimsby for Goldborough's return, because they chose to serve her the rest of their lives.

Swiftly Grim's sons set their house in order. They pulled up their boats, all but the longboat they meant to take with them for the journey, and stored them in the squat boathouses whose roofs came down to the ground.

They saw to it that their sisters had plenty of food in

the storehouse, and wood against the winter, if they should be gone so long. They put Solvi in charge of their fields and marketing. Hild offered to help with the milking and the cheese-making.

Robert the Red saw to the turf on the hall roof and the thatch on the out-buildings, to be sure they were storm proof and well weighted against the wind.

Havelok helped with all of these tasks, doing the work of two strong men. Goldborough helped with the work of the house and the garden, her fair hair braided and bound about her head beneath a fine, white cloth, as befitted a wedded woman.

In this fashion Grim's sons prepared to set forth with Havelok and Goldborough to win back a kingdom.

xiv

Horda and Godrich

Now the day that Havelok took Goldborough away with him, men trod softly at Godrich's court, against the wrath of the Earl. He was surly and easily angered, as he sat bitter-mooded in his high seat. He was angry at himself over this ill-conceived wedding, knowing that the princess he had planned to humble with a baseborn husband had gone off with no churlish lump from the kitchen, but a man who looked every inch a king.

Godrich squirmed as he thought of the crown that had been placed on Goldborough's fair hair. He hoped that his nobles had not noted how it became her regal beauty. He thought of the old chest and of how the serving people had staggered beneath its weight. What a fool he had been not to have checked into that long since. Who would have thought–

He clapped his hands. "Send me Solvi and the serving woman, Hild," he ordered.

"They are gone, My Lord." The knees of the thrall who spoke were shaking.

"Gone!" shouted Earl Godrich. "Gone where?"

"I do not know, My Lord. To Wales they say. They left at once, after the wedding."

"Since when has a thrall the right to leave this court without asking?"

"Solvi said the Princess had given him the right to take the thrall-ring from his neck. He had it in writing from the old king. He had promised her father to serve her until the time she was wed. And Hild the same. The paper said she was Goldborough's serving maid, and not bound to any other."

Godrich was furious. He rose and struck the man again and again, beating him with his hands over face and head, or anywhere the man could not shield himself. "Get out, you muttonhead!" he shouted. "Bring me the chest that lies in Goldborough's room."

The man still held his arms to shield his head as he stumbled to the door. "The chest too is gone, My Lord," he said in a hoarse voice. "They took it with them, on the horse that belongs to the Princess."

He dodged out the door as Godrich picked up a heavy candlestick, and threw it with deadly aim. It crashed to the earth floor of the penthouse, and skidded into the garth beyond.

No one came to pick it up.

Earl Godrich trembled and shook with the anger that raged in him. He strode out into the yard and shouted.

The servants came, all unwilling, because the man who had been beaten warned them that Earl Godrich was beside himself. "He is like to have a fit in his fury," he told them. "It will go hard with anyone who crosses his path."

The Earl sent men along all the roads on his fastest horses, to seek the two servants and the chest. But they knew that there was slim chance of their finding the runaways. Truth to tell they did not much care.

That evening there came to the court the man named Horda. He had a train of servants and hangers-on in his following. Earl Godrich had given this man, in exchange for money and goods, a castle and lands which the young Earl of Chester claimed as his own. Reyner of Chester had protested the gift of his lands to this Dane from overseas. Earl Godrich had been forced to set this matter before the Parliament to be judged.

He had forgotten that the suit was set for hearing in a few days' time. It did not improve his temper that he must needs marshal his wits and use his utmost power to swing this matter to his liking.

He greeted Horda grudgingly. He brought him to his table and sat him beside the high seat. He sent for meat and drink.

The wedding candles had burned down. The heavy hand-hewn boards of the tables stretched away from the hearth fire into the gloom.

Horda was dressed in rich clothes, but they were dirty and travel-stained. The fur that edged his tunic looked bedraggled and mangy. He scratched the matted hair on his chest as he ate, and when food or drink spilled in his beard, he wiped it off with a careless hand.

When he had eaten his fill he belched heartily, and leaned back. He patted his full paunch, blowing out his cheeks. "It is a long ride from that moldy castle," he complained. "I would have done better to have bargained for something closer."

Earl Godrich wanted to shout at him that he was glad to have him as far off as possible, but he curbed his ill will. After all, he thought, this slovenly Norseman has money from somewhere. Money is not so easy found these days.

"We will be lucky if you can keep it," he said, sourly. "The men of the Parliament are none too eager to see our holdings go to outlanders."

"If I lose it," said Horda, glancing at Godrich with his crafty eyes, "you will have to find me another—or pay back the money you owe me. No one gets something for nothing these days." He took out a long, thin knife from a sheath at his belt, to dig out a piece of meat from a front tooth. He did not put the knife back but laid it beside his plate, which was heaped with bones. With a quick gesture he gathered up the greasy bones and flung them to the dogs that sniffed about the table.

"The money has been spent," said Godrich shortly.

Horda shrugged. "Then you will give me other lands. But it should not be too difficult to see that the Parliament casts its vote in my favor. I do not want trouble with the Earl of Chester, or your Thing men either, over this matter." He looked about at the empty board where he and Godrich sat by themselves. "Where are they all gone? Do your people not eat with you?"

"They ate earlier. There was a wedding." Earl Godrich stirred restlessly, his anger rising again within him. "There was a small wedding feast after." He laughed shortly. "The wedding party was in haste and did not wait for food."

Horda looked about the room idly, noting the rich hangings, the jeweled weapons, the spoons of beaten silver. His beady eyes appraised the fur rugs on the floor and knew to a penny what they would bring.

Godrich watched him warily.

"Who was it then," asked Horda, not really caring, "who must wed in such haste?"

"My ward, the Princess Goldborough," answered Godrich, banging his fist down on the table at the remembrance of it.

"Ho!" This was of interest to Horda. Goldborough was the heir to Athelwold, the King. Perhaps there was something here that might be turned to good account. She must have lands and goods, this princess, if not all of England.

Godrich was staring into his wine cup, lost in angry thought.

Horda leaned forward. "To what man did you give the Princess, Godrich, and so save something for yourself?" He winked knowingly at the Earl.

Earl Godrich shook off his thoughts and gave a sickly grin, pursing his lips after it. "I gave her to a lowborn cook's helper, a kitchen knave."

Horda slapped his thigh with a resounding smack. "Hoo! Hoo!" he crowed. "England will never crown a lowborn king."

Godrich felt better. "I am not forsworn either," he boasted. "I swore on the Holy Book to give her to the strongest, and fairest man I could find. Could I help it if this should be a man with grease on his hands and splinters in his fingers?"

"Where have they got to?" asked Horda, chuckling in his beard.

Earl Godrich shrugged. "I do not know or care. They set out on foot, and I let them go. I am freed of this charge, and now she can fend for herself."

"It might be better to get her still farther out of your way," suggested Horda. "He cannot bite who is safe beneath the sod."

"No. I do not want her blood upon my hands. She has had some of the earls clamoring before this for her release from the seacoast tower. This Reyner of Chester who claims your fee, and some of the others as well."

Horda grunted.

"Besides," said the Earl, wincing at the thought of it, "the man she married is to be reckoned with. He is not such a stupid ox as I thought."

"Surely you can spare enough men to bring him down."

"Of course I can. But then too many would have knowledge of this business. It is better to wait for a time on this."

"Where does this kitchen knave hail from?

"From north of here on the coast. His people are fisherfolk. From somewhere he has learned wrestling and putting the stone. It came to my ears when he won over all the champions at the Fair this week. He is a giant of a man."

Horda was thinking that it might be a good idea to get hold of this princess and her strong man. It would be a sword to hold over Godrich. He could see that. Thoughts began to churn in his mind, around and around until there

was a path as well worn as though made by an ox turning a mill rock.

Godrich sat staring into his wine glass.

"What is he called, this giant?" asked Horda.

"His name is Havelok. Grim's son—"

Horda leapt to his feet as though someone had pricked his fat rump with a knife point. "By the blood of Odin—you fool! You deep-dyed fool!"

Earl Godrich sprang up, livid with fury. "Mind your tongue!" he shouted. "No one calls me fool—"

Horda fell back in his chair, his face white and pasty from shock.

Godrich stared at him, a fierce fear gripping him. "Who is he?" he asked hoarsely. "What have I done?"

"Havelok!" Horda spat out the name. "Havelok! The whole of England to choose from, and you choose Havelok. You nithing! He is no kitchen churl. This giant of a kitchen knave is Birkabeyn's son, and right-born king of the Danes."

"After them!" screamed Godrich. He ran from the room, frothing at the mouth, and kicking the dogs out of his way. He shouted at his men to bring horses. He was like a madman, dancing and gibbering, laying the flat of his sword on all who dared to come near him.

Horda sat where he was at the empty board, stroking his wine-stained beard. He was thinking, thinking. His mind was snuffling in all the corners of this business, like a rat nosing about in a store room. Somewhere in all this matter there should be something he could get his teeth into.

He sauntered out into the courtyard. "Where will you hunt them?" he asked Godrich. "Grimsby?"

"I must get men first," said Godrich. "I came north with too few men. The earls will come with me or lose their lands. We will harry all England until we rout her out."

Horda watched them go. Then he sent for his men and his horse and rode from the castle.

"Where to, Master?" asked his Captain.

"Home first. Then we ride to Grimsby," answered Horda absently.

But when they came to Grimsby there were only two women there and a few well-armed servants.

"Our menfolk have gone fishing," said Gunnild. She spread her hands regretfully. "They will not be back until they have a good catch."

There was nothing that Horda could do about that.

xv

Denmark

Whether the journey was long or short for the sailing of Havelok and Goldborough and the three Grim's sons, when they landed in Denmark they journeyed until they reached the castle of a Danish Jarl named Ubbe. This Jarl had been a good friend to King Birkabeyn in years gone by. He was a justice. Havelok had heard from men of good will that Jarl Ubbe was fair and honest in all his dealings.

Havelok found him a strong, broad man of forty winters, with a spade-cut beard more gray than black. He had dark eyebrows above wide-set eyes that were as gray-blue as a Pictish agate. To him Havelok offered the jeweled pin that Grim had saved for him, the pin that had been fastened to his cloak when Grim opened the black sack with a boy inside of it.

Ubbe saw the value of this fibula and the Danish workmanship of it. He wondered at it, and about the man who offered such a princely gift.

"May I have your leave, Jarl Ubbe, to sell my wares

from one town to another here in Denmark?" asked Havelok.

Jarl Ubbe saw that this young man who stood before him was long-bodied and strong, well-knit and thick-breasted. He seemed better, he thought, for the bearing of shield and spear, for knighthood, than for selling goods. Memory teased at him, he was so sure he had seen this youth before. He wanted to see more of this tall Englander who spoke Danish as though his tongue had been long used to the sounds of it.

"You shall have this boon," he told Havelok, "if you will come to dine with me and bring your good wife."

Havelok feared there might be some danger to Goldborough, but Jarl Ubbe called after him, "Mind that you come, you hear?" Havelok did not dare refuse.

When he told the Princess of the Jarl's request, she was well pleased. "I shall wear my blue dress and walk proud. Then these Dane men will say surely this peddler's wife is nobly born. Besides I have a mind to see what a Danish home is like, since I have wedded me such an uncouth Dane."

Then Havelok snatched her white coif from her head, and rumpled her fair hair all about her face, until both of them were weak from laughter.

Ubbe's mead-hall was larger than Havelok had ever seen. In the stone-lined hearth down the center three fires burned, with glowing turf coals heaped up between them. The pillars holding up the high roof were fair-carved, writhing with birds and beasts and scrolls all intertwined. The doors of the wall beds at the far end were also carved, and bright with paint and gilt.

Before the wide benches were tables set with colored linen stitched in gold, and wooden and silver plates. Candles were tied to branching antlers or stood on painted wheels hung from the high rafters. Torches smoked and sputtered in holders on the walls. Painted shields hung against the tapestries, with other war gear. Most of these were finely worked and glittered with gems.

A gleeman thrummed a harp. A few children played about with the shaggy dogs that lay on the rush-strewn floor. In this well-ordered household both dogs and children were quiet and mannerly.

Havelok and Goldborough went down the long hall to where Jarl Ubbe sat in his high seat. Havelok walked before her with measured tread. Beside her walked Robert the Red, who would have given his life before any harm befell her. On the other side of her was William Wendut. Behind her, his eyes darting here and there at the wonder of it, strode Hugh Raven, blood-brother to Havelok.

In this manner Goldborough walked like the high-born lady she was, in a ring of goodly men, with Havelok standing over them like a tall tree.

At the sight of them, as they drew near the high seat, Jarl Ubbe and his men rose and waited for them.

When it was time to eat, Ubbe brought in his own wife. He said, half in jest, "Lady, thou and Havelok shall share a plate, and Goldborough with me."

The blessing was asked. Then all manner of good food was brought in by the serving carls, food fit for a king. Swans and venison, lampreys and peacocks were set before them, with spiced wine, and Rhineland wines both white and red.

Ubbe was thinking to himself, if I let these young people go on their way to sell their goods, there will surely be trouble because of this woman. For her sake men would gladly kill her lord.

So he called forth ten knights and sixty men with bows and lances. He sent Havelok and Goldborough with them the next day to a magistrate of the town named Bernard Brown. He bade this man guard the visitors as he would his own life.

Bernard Brown welcomed them and prepared rich fare for them. But just as they were about to dine, sixty men with drawn swords and spears came, demanding entrance to the house. "Open the door!" they shouted.

Hearing the shouts, the magistrate started up. He cast on his byrnie, seized an ax and leapt to the door. "Who comes?" he shouted. "Who are you to thus disturb my peace?"

A man outside heaved up a boulder and flung it with all his strength. It split the door asunder.

When Havelok saw this, he drew out the great iron bar that held the door. "Come then, you scum. Cursed be he who flees."

Then one of the men drew his sword and three of them set upon Havelok to kill him. Havelok lifted up the bar and with one blow he slew all three of them. A fourth he knocked down with a blow on the head. Another he smote between the shoulder blades as he turned to flee.

When he had struck down two more, the rest backed away. They divided into two companies, to rush on him

from two sides at once, like dogs on a cornered bear. They were strong and quick and soon they had wounded him in many places.

Seeing how the blood ran from his wounds, Havelok was as maddened as a berserker. With the great iron bar he struck at them. A great din arose, a shouting and howling. They stood far off from him, not daring to come closer. They hurled stones at him and spears.

Hugh Raven heard the shouts and cries. He was afraid that Havelok might be in danger. Catching up an oar, he hurried to the struggle in the dooryard. He saw how the thieves fought against Havelok, six to one.

"Woe!" he cried. "Robert! William! Where are ye? Help us! Get bars and strike these dogs or our lord will die. Quick! Follow me. I have an oar!"

Robert the Red caught up a strong staff that could easily bear a net. William Wendut took a bar greater than his thigh. The magistrate, Bernard Brown, had his ax.

Like madmen they leapt into the fray. They fell upon the thieves, with Havelok beside them, and smote them hip and thigh. They struck them down until not one of them was left alive. When morning came and it was day, the intruders lay in heaps upon the steps. They were dragged off to the fields and left in the furrows.

When the tidings of the struggle came to Ubbe, the Jarl called his knights to him. They armed themselves and rode to the magistrate's house.

Bernard Brown came out to them, sore-wounded and his clothing all but struck off of him. "Lord!" he cried to Ubbe. "More than sixty robbers came here in the night. They broke down my door and would have killed me, if

Havelok had not come to my aid. With the heavy door-tree he drove the dogs out."

He paused for breath and Ubbe urged him on.

"A thousand men is this man worth alone. I should be dead by now except for his strength and valor. But he is sore-hurt. They gave him more than twenty wounds, the least of which could easily be his bane."

"Bring Havelok to me quickly, that I may set a leech to tend his wounds," said Ubbe. "If he can be healed I myself will make him a knight for this night's work.

They brought Havelok to Jarl Ubbe. When the leech had seen to Havelok's wounds and said they would soon be healed, the Jarl ceased his moan.

"Come with me," Ubbe said to Havelok, "with your wife and serving men. I will stand between you and the friends of those you have slain. No man shall lie in wait to do you harm. I will bring you to a room in my own high tower. I shall lie close at hand. I and my knights will guard you, and no hurt shall come to your lady."

They rode to the Jarl's castle. He housed them in a high tower. Robert the Red and William Wendut and Hugh Raven slept outside of the door to the room, to guard it. Ubbe and his knights slept in a lower room.

In the middle of the night Jarl Ubbe was wakened by a light as bright as day. Fearing thieves or some other treachery, he peered through a crack.

All three of Grim's sons were asleep, but from inside the room where Havelok lay there was a gleam of sunlight coming from his mouth, shining bright as he slept.

The Jarl called his knights and men. "Come quietly and look on this thing," he told them. Because the brightness was as though a hundred and seven candles burned in that room.

On Havelok's shoulder they could see a cross that was a king's mark, clear and as bright as gold in the light. Sparkling it shone like a red jewel, giving enough light of its own to choose a penny by.

Then all who were there, both high and low, knew that Havelok was a king's son.

"This is surely Birkabeyn's heir!" cried Ubbe. "This man is as like the King as brother might be to brother."

The knights pushed their way up the stairs and into the room, holding off Grim's sons who would have stopped them. They fell at Havelok's feet and kissed them, with much weeping and laughter.

Havelok woke. At first he was angered. He feared this was another band of thieves come to kill all of them.

Then Jarl Ubbe said, "Have no fear, Lord. We wish only good to her and you. I come to offer my homage. In very truth, from now on I will be your man. We know now that you are the son of Birkabeyn, our lawful king. Tomorrow all the jarls and barons, warriors and thanes shall come to do you homage. I shall have the greatest joy in making you a knight.

Havelok was blithe at this. He thanked God with all his heart.

In the morning when it was light, Jarl Ubbe sent word to all his people of both low and high degree to come before him. He sent thanes riding with this message, "Come, as you love your own lives and those of your wives and children."

No man dared to disobey this summons. When they

had come and were assembled at the place of the Thing, Jarl Ubbe stood up before all of them.

A horn blew a high thin silvery note. All those sitting on the hillside rose. The talk-murmur was hushed. It was a windy morning, and sunny. The wind caught at the Jarl's fine gray hair, twisting it in a tangle above his head.

"Listen to what I will tell you." The Jarl's voice rang from one side of the half circle to the other. "You all know full well how all of Denmark was Birkabeyn's land and we his men."

They shouted at this, and clashed their spears against their shield rims. There was not a man there who did not have cause for sorrow that the days of Birkabeyn were gone.

"You know how he, by your counsel, gave over his three children, Havelok, his heir, and his two daughters, and all of his lands and goods into Jarl Godard's hands."

There was a murmuring and a muttering at this. A deep groan rose and fell.

"On the Holy Book Jarl Godard swore to care for these motherless children. But he forgot his sacred oath. He slew the maidens, Helfled and Swanborough. He would have killed the boy as well, if God had not stayed his hand."

There was silence now, as they leaned forward to catch every word.

"Jarl Godard gave this boy to Grim, the fisherman, to be drowned. By the mark on his shoulder Grim knew this boy to be king-born. He fled from Denmark with his wife and children, and made his way to England. For many winters he fed and fostered Havelok. Now look upon this young man. Can any of you who ever knew Birkabeyn say that this is not Birkabeyn's son?"

"No!" they shouted. "No!" and the shield rims rang.

"Be glad of this strong youth," said Jarl Ubbe, stilling the tumult with a raised hand. "Come hither and give homage to your lord. I myself will be the first."

Ubbe, bare-headed, fell to his knees. He placed his hands in Havelok's hands. He spoke out loud and clear, so that all who were there could hear him. "I promise in the name of God and Christ to be Havelok's man all the days of my life, and to defend him against all others."

Havelok raised him from his knees and kissed him on both cheeks. All could see how Jarl Ubbe had become Havelok's man. After him came the jarls, and every baron in that town, all the knights and thanes and common men. At the day's end there was not one from whom Havelok had not had sworn fealty.

When all had been sworn, Jarl Ubbe sent men to bring out his high seat from his hall. Ubbe sat in the seat where all could see him. He placed Havelok on the footboard below him. Then he took a sword, sun-bright and jeweled. He dubbed Havelok knight, bidding him rise and sit in the high seat in his own right, as King of all Denmark.

The *thingstead* and the woods behind and the very sky itself rang with the joy of the Dane men.

For two days there was feasting and games, with fights of all kinds. Spear fights and buckler play, bull and boar fighting, and the terrible contests of wild stallions brought in from the woods. There was wrestling and stone-putting, harping and piping and the singing of old tales. There was gift giving and plenty of good food.

As soon as he was made king, Havelok knighted Robert the Red and William Wendut and Hugh Raven. He made them all three barons. He gave them lands and castles with twenty knights and many serving people, both men and women.

When the feasting was finished the King kept one thousand knights and five thousand men.

Before they set out to do battle with Godard, Goldborough brought to Havelok a byrnie of tough horsehide on which she had sewn iron rings. When she helped him on with it she said, "Put on this war-woof, king's son. It has been proved against all but stone."

"I will dodge the stones," he told her, laughing. For a long, sweet moment he held her face between his hands.

They set out to meet Jarl Godard, knowing that the Jarl must have had word of their coming by this time. They met Godard's men in full war array, in a valley by the sea.

Robert the Red, who was master of the army, was the first to come upon Godard. He cried out to him, "Come then, Jarl, give homage to your king."

Godard struck him a mighty blow with his fist. Robert the Red seized his long knife and smote the Jarl through the arm.

Godard's men fell back when they saw all the horde of Danes pouring down the hill. Godard shouted at them. "Cowards! Are you knights? I have fed all of you, and will again, if you will help me now in this time of need. Shame on you if you let this impostor work his will."

Then his men rallied and went forward. They killed one of the King's knights and wounded many others.

Havelok's men sent up a mighty shout at this. They fell upon Godard's men and killed all of them but their chief. They bound Godard fast, though he struggled and roared like a bull. They threw him upon a scurvy mare with his feet to the tail, and brought him to Havelok.

"Old sin makes new shame!" said Havelok sternly. "You shall pay now for the ancient wrong you wrought against me and mine."

The King called Jarl Ubbe and all the men of his army together on the hill. "It is for you to speak this man's doom," he told them.

Sitting around in a great circle, the lords gave true judgment. "We doom that Godard shall be flayed, drawn to the gallows on this wretched horse, and hanged. It shall be written there, 'This is the wicked man who thought to take from our rightful King his land, and who killed the King's sisters.' The doom is doomed."

When Godard was shriven by the priest this dreadful doom was carried out.

Now after Jarl Godard was dead, the King took all of his land and houses and goods and gave them to Jarl Ubbe. "Here I give you power over all this land in fee. At Grimsby, because of the good that Grim did me so long ago, giving me aid and food and fostering through the years, I will make a priory of monks to serve Christ there until Doomsday."

Then Havelok and Goldborough took homage from all in Denmark and gathered ships and stores and weapons, with knights and men at arms and women who were glad to go with them and serve Havelok's queen.

The sea swarmed with the dragon ships, all of them fresh-painted with yellow paint, their red eyes glaring balefully and their tongues dripping, as they set sail for England.

xvi

Two Crowns

It was a fair day when the first of the dragon ships nosed its way up the broad reach of the Humber. Havelok stood in the prow as Grim had stood many years before. Behind him were his three foster brothers. The rowers bent to the oars with the rhythm sung by the helmsman. The great striped sail above them nattered and creaked as the light wind puffed against it.

Behind them came the fleet of ships. In the middle of the fleet was a longship with the best armed and strongest knights guarding Goldborough and her women.

Fires burned on the hills above Grimsby. On the beach where the wooden dock ran down to the river stood Gunnild, tall and strong. Her hair was in gold braids to her knees, her gray eyes were shining with pleasure at their safe return. Behind her was Levive, misty-eyed and slender-fingered, gentle and a little shy before all these strangers. Her lips were trembling with joy.

In his haste to greet them, Havelok stumbled from the ship and fell to his knees. A great shout went up at this, from his own ship and those that followed, since this was thought to be sign of good luck.

"Truly I had never thought to see you again!" Levive cried, hugging her brothers and Havelok.

Gunnild and Levive took Goldborough to the hall to rest after the long hard journey. They made up her bed with soft skins and the smoothest linen, and found bedding places for her women.

That night the wayfarers learned all the news of the farm while they had been gone. Gunnild and Levive were more than glad to welcome them home. There had been a matter of much concern to them the last months.

"It is the man, Horda," they explained.

"He has been here many times, seeking marriage with Gunnild," said Levive. "We held him off, saying that such a serious matter must wait until our brothers returned."

Robert the Red was growling with anger.

"This last time," said Gunnild, "he said that he would take the matter to Earl Godrich. He said that the Earl would force us to consent, or he would take our farm and boats and all that we have."

"Is he here?" demanded Havelok.

"No," answered Levive. "He took horse for Lincoln when the fires were lit on the hills that meant the dragon ships had been sighted."

"Then by this time Godrich knows that we have come back," said Robert the Red. "This time we will settle this Horda once and for all."

Gunnild and Levive told the home-comers of the crops and the sales of butter and cheese. They told of two colts fighting in the kitchen, with Gunnild struggling with one and Hild with the other, while Levive whacked away at all of them with the straw besom.

In the morning, Goldborough came to Gunnild and Levive bearing in her arms a silken dress shimmering and flame-colored. "Help me, sisters," she begged of them. "We need a banner for this battle."

The women cut and stitched on the silken stuff. They embroidered on it, for all to see, two golden crowns linked and locked together. They took the tiny, sparkling buttons that had run down the dress front, and sewed them like jewels to the points of the two crowns. They laughed at this foolishness, but all the time their eyes were sick with fear of the coming battle.

Goldborough gave the brave and glittering banner to William Wendut. He made a pole and crossbar to hang it on. He swore in Christ's name to hold it against all comers on the highest hill.

When Godrich of Cornwall learned from Horda that Havelok was now King of Denmark, and that Goldborough, the fair and rightful heir to the throne of England, was at Grimsby, he was both angry and sorrowful. Quickly he called forth for the army every man who could ride a horse or bear a weapon.

"Come to Lincoln," he bade them, "by the seventeenth of March. If there be any who rebel, by Christ and St. John I will make him and his children thralls."

The English were afraid of Earl Godrich. They came flocking into the city on the day that had been set.

When they were assembled Godrich stood up before them. "Listen!" he cried. "I have called you forth from your homes for good reason. Strangers have come to Grimsby on the coast. They are Norsemen who mean to burn your homes and steal your women. A man named Havelok leads them. He has burned the churches and killed both priests and nuns."

They mumbled and growled at this and he let them have their say.

"If this Havelok rules that part of England now, soon he will be here to kill all of us and make us slaves."

They shouted their anger.

"Let us march against these marauders," screamed Godrich. "We must kill them like the dogs they are. We must drive them from the land."

They shouted that they were ready to fight with him.

"Follow me, for I will be first to strike him down with my drawn sword. Cursed be he who stands not fast beside me."

"Yea! Yea!" shouted most of them.

Earl Reyner of Chester turned to a man who stood beside him. This was a slight and wiry, gray-haired man, with sea-blue eyes like glacial ice in a leathery face. He had a sidewise slant to his lips. "When one dog begins to bark, the rest join in," said the Earl. "Is this Havelok the man you spoke of, Singer?"

"Yes." The small man stooped to pick up his long staff and to ease the harp that hung on his back. "Have I your leave, Master, to seek him out?"

"Go with God's blessing, Pakkanen. Bid him look to his arms."

While the rest of the host milled about, the slim, dark man took off between the hedgerows. He was whistling between his teeth, swinging along at a steady dog trot. When he was well out of the city, his stride lengthened until he was running in a tireless lope that ate up the miles between Lincoln and Grimsby.

Behind him men were buckling on their bright byrnies and helmets. Those who had horses gathered on the common. The rest were marshaled in some sort of order on the plowed acres below the town.

From all sides they came, girding on their war harness from jackets of willow withes bound with bull hide, to the shining mail of the knights. Each man took what he had, swords and spears and battle axes for the gentle-born, scythes and sickles and boathooks for the common folk.

When they were gathered and armed, the horsemen led the way. The rest came trooping after.

In the meantime Havelok was delighted to welcome Pakkanen. He gathered him in his arms and hugged him until Pakkanen shouted that his ribs were cracking.

Pakkanen rejoiced to see the tall, comely man this boy had become, a proper warrior and a leader of men. From him Havelok learned each thing about Godrich and the start of the army the Earl had gathered so hastily.

Havelok called his men. He set them in battle array, with the red banner higher-most on a hill overlooking the road to Lincoln. Men planted stakes there and dug trenches in front of them, to trap the horses if the English should choose to ride against them.

Havelok and all three of Grim's sons and Jarl Ubbe had horses. The rest of the Danes were afoot. Havelok saw to it that all his men were well armed, and that they carried food and water. The Danes wore byrnies covered with iron rings or shell flakes sewn on, each overlapping the next, like fish scales. On their heads were helmets of hide or burnished iron, with spreading horns or eagle wings.

It was early the next day when the two armies came together. The army of Earl Godrich was three times as large as Havelok's band of Danish knights. But they were not war-skilled like the Danes, and many were poorly armed.

As the war horns roared and the pipes squealed, Havelok struck off the head of the first knight he met. Robert the Red killed another. Sword clashed against sword and the shields clanged. Men found that daggers and long knives were better than spears or javelins for the fierce infighting.

The bowmen and the stone slingers held off, since they could not tell which were their own men in the press. They took their short and heavy saxes to join in the fighting.

High on the hill the flame-colored banner dipped and rose. The silk bellied out in the wind so all could see the jeweled crowns. A great shout came rolling down the hillslope like the rumble of thunder before a storm. All the Danes took heart from those two crowns floating in the wind.

Above the shouts could be heard the neighing of frightened horses, the clamor of beaten shield rims, and the screams of wounded men. The dust rose in clouds until the sun looked through it blood-red. It was a bitter choking for those who must fight in it.

Jarl Ubbe came upon Earl Godrich. The battle between

them was grim. They fought until both were struck from their horses. Then they drew swords. They fought in fury all through the day until sunset.

At last Godrich gave Ubbe such a deadly stroke that he would have fallen, if Hugh Raven had not caught him up on his horse and carried him from the field of battle.

Before Ubbe was rescued a thousand knights had been slain. There was no counting the common soldiers lying dead or wounded on the hill.

In a fever of rage Godrich rushed at the Danes. He mowed them down like grass beneath a scythe.

When Havelok saw how his people died, he was filled with anger. He drove his horse into the thickest of the battle, where he found Godrich striking men down on all sides.

"Godrich!" shouted Havelok. "Have done with this killing. You know full well that Athelwold made you swear on the Holy Book that you would give England to his daughter when she came of age to rule. Yield to her now with no more bloodshed. I will forgive you all injury to her and me, for I see how great is your strength and valor."

"Never!" shouted Godrich. With his sword in both hands he struck such a mighty blow that he cut Havelok's rim-circled shield in two.

Havelok was blind with fury over this shame done him in front of all his army. He beat Godrich down to the earth. The Earl started up and struck at Havelok. The grievous blow cut through whole rings of Havelok's byrnie and pierced his side.

Havelok, pain-maddened, gathered all his strength. He

heaved high his 'Thorn of the Shields' and struck off Godrich's sword hand.

Then he bound the traitor in fetters and sent him to the Queen. "He is a knight," he commanded his men. "No

one shall strike him or do him shame until the knights have doomed him."

The English, seeing their leader bound, laid down their arms. As suddenly as it started, the battle-flame was quenched. In the hush that followed the shouting and clanging, the dust and the bloodshed, there came the trilling of a wood thrush in a hawthorn tree, and the gray scent of crushed mint underfoot.

Hugh Raven came to stand beside Havelok. He was stanching a wound in his arm with a torn sleeve. His eyes were twinkling. "I'm *s-starved!*" he said, with a grin.

During the last of the battle there had been trouble at the home place. Havelok had left Pakkanen there, in charge of a handful of well-armed men, to guard Grim's daughters and the Queen.

Horda had thought to himself that there would not be men enough to guard the women. He had persuaded his serving men to go with him to Grimsby. "We can hold the Queen of the Danes for ransom money," he told them. "Gunnild Grimsdatter is for me. The rest of the women you can have when we have sacked and burned the hall."

His men were willing, seeing that the battle was going against them. They followed the path by the stream, which was running red now, with the blood of the slain of both armies.

Pakkanen was on watch. He saw the small band of men creeping through the orchard trees. He gave a shout and sprang down from the loft to join the Danes. He set them to guard the hall, and helped the women up the loft ladder. He returned to the door of the fore-porch, a battle ax in his hand.

Horda rode into the garth. "Heil Finn!" he shouted.

"Grave robber!" answered Pakkanen.

Horda could not see the men within the hall. He thought Pakkanen alone guarded the women. He laughed as he set spurs to his horse, thinking to ride the Finn down where he stood on the stone in the dooryard.

Pakkanen dodged back into the doorway, as slick and quick as a red fox. As the horse swerved he caught the stirrup and ran beside the beast. He dropped his ax and plunged the long knife from his belt into the side of the horse. The heavy animal reared and plunged to his knees. Horda was thrown on the hard earth of the garth.

Pakkanen was on him like a cat. As the Dane men ran out to meet Horda's troop, the Finn caught the Norseman by the throat.

Pakkanen was half the size of the man on the ground. It looked to be an uneven battle, especially to Horda. He gave a bellow of laughter as he reached his big hands up to crush the man who stood over him.

Pakkanen caught one hand and twisted it. Horda gave a yelp of pain. He struggled to get away from the Finn. Pakkanen let him roll and rolled with him. Then he brought up the hand he held with a quick pull.

Horda let out a screech of agony. He kicked out viciously. But Pakkanen was up now, dancing about like a puppet on a string. He danced in and out, too quick for Horda to reach him or to strike at him.

The Finn snatched up Horda's battle ax from the ground. He danced off, turned, and sent the gleaming ax spinning end over end. It cut through the metal helmet and Horda lay still.

Pakkanen stood over him panting, not listening to the sounds of struggle behind him. Deliberately he gathered spit in his dry mouth. He spat on the ground and smeared it into the earth with his foot. "Spit for spit, grave robber," he said. "But you will take nothing of mine with you where you go, save the ax-blow that finished you."

A young cockerel crowed a squeaky, broken crow from the dunghill beyond the stable. Pakkanen shouted with laughter. He tossed his ax in the air and caught it behind his back. "I too can strut," he called to the young cock. He turned back to help the Dane men.

Horda's men had seen their leader fall. They turned to flee with the Danes after them.

"We watched from the smoke hole, Pakkanen," said Gunnild breathlessly. "How could you beat down a man as big as that?"

Pakkanen laughed. "I learned a few tricks in my tumbling days. He who travels alone has need of a trick or two. I could not have done this to Horda, perhaps, before he robbed the grave ship. He was soft and pot-bellied from that sin, and easy enough to twist in my fingers."

When the English learned that Goldborough was England's rightful heir, and that Havelok, the King of Denmark, had wedded her, they cried for his mercy and hers. They offered him homage.

Havelok would take nothing from them until the Queen was brought. Six jarls rode off to Grimsby after her, and brought her back with them.

When she stood before them, all could see what a peerless, gracious lady this was. She came dressed in the soft blue dress of her wedding day, with amber beads about her neck. On her head was the golden fillet, with the stone that matched her eyes. Beneath the slender, twisted crown she wore a head-cloth of snowy white, made of Gunnild's finest linen thread, all edged with gold.

The English fell on their knees before their lady, sore-weeping. "Christ's mercy and yours," they cried to her. "All of England shall be yours, and we your men. Not one of us, young or old, but knows that Athelwold was king and you his heir."

Then Havelok stood before them. "It is for you now to sit down as doomsmen over Godrich. See that you judge him as he deserves, for justice spares no man, no matter what his rank. Then if you wish and counsel it, the Queen and I will take your homage."

None dared hinder the doom. Gathered in a doom-ring, the knights condemned Godrich to be bound to a worthless ass, with his head to the tail, and clothed in shameful dress. He was to be led to a green in the midst of Lincoln. There he was to be bound to a stake and burnt to dust. This doom was quickly done.

Havelok and Goldborough took homage from all the English.

Then Havelok called to him Reyner, the Earl of Chester, a young, unmarried knight. Pakkanen had told him that this earl had sent the word to Grimsby about the arming of the English, and when they would march.

"Sir Earl," said Havelok, "if you will take my counsel, I will do well by you. By St. John I will give you for wife the fairest thing alive beside the Queen. She is Gunnild, my foster sister, daughter of Grim, who fled with me from Denmark to save me from death. I counsel that you marry her, for she is fair and glad-hearted. There is none her match in all England for the skill of her weaving. She is very dear to me. For her sake you, too, will be dear to me."

The Earl would do nothing against the King. When

Gunnild saw Reyner of Chester, and knew him for a kindly man, and learned how he had been of help to Havelok, she consented to this wedding. It is said of these two that they had five sons, all of whom were dear to Havelok.

Havelok did not forget Bertram, the Earl's cook. "For the good you did me in my need, friend, you shall receive rich reward. For when I went in my coat of sailcloth from Grim's house, and had no bread nor anything of my own, you did feed me and clothe me well. When I had need of a weapon, you gave me the true sword, 'Thorn of the Shields.'"

Bertram waited, smiling at Havelok.

"Have for that kindness, now," the king went on, "the Earldom of Cornwall, and all Godrich's land in town and field. Moreover, if she will have you, I would that you marry Grim's daughter, Levive. She knows well how to save men's lives, and to blunt the edges of their anger. She is courteous and as fair as a rose that opens to the sun. She is a skilled housewife and can turn her hand to all womanly tasks."

Then Havelok girded Bertram with the sword of the Earldom. With his own hand he made him a knight. He gave him arms and wedded him to that sweet maid, Levive.

Havelok feasted his Danes and gave them many lands and goods. Soon after this he and Goldborough went south to London for his crowning and hers. The feast of the crowning lasted with great joy for forty days or more.

When he saw that the Danes were ready to fare back to Denmark, Havelok gave them leave to go. He commanded that Jarl Ubbe should be his head-man in Denmark so that no complaint should come to him.

Robert the Red chose to go back to Denmark with Jarl Ubbe. He became Ubbe's right-hand man, and a Jarl high in the Council-ring at the *thingstead,* guarding the Danish rights of Havelok.

William Wendut returned to Grimsby where he could farm and fish and work with wood and metal and stone, to his heart's content. He and his men were ready whenever Havelok had need of them.

Hugh Raven married the girl he had known in Grimsby. Havelok gave them lands and castles. But Hugh Raven stayed at the court, to guard with his life and aid with his counsel his blood-brother and the Queen.

Havelok ruled England and Denmark for sixty years, with Goldborough. All the world spoke of these two, and of their great love. Neither one was joyous away from the other, and their love was always new.

They bore fifteen sons and daughters, of whom God willed that each should be a king or queen.

Pakkanen, the Finn, stayed with Havelok to sing in his court. "I am tired of the road dust and the sea salt," he told Havelok. "Besides that, I have a new song to sing. It is a tale of treachery and woe, of bright love and two crowns that intertwine. I would sing it to your children, king's son."

Bibliography

Anglo-Saxon Chronicle (Chas. Plummer, *ed.*)

Ashe, Geoffrey
From Caesar to Arthur 1960

Barnard, Francis Pierrepont
Mediaeval England

Beda, Venerabilis
The Venerable Bede's Ecclesiastical History of England

Bell, Alexander, *ed.*
Le Lai d'Haveloc and
Gaimar's Haveloc Episode 1925

Blair, P. Hunter
Introduction to Anglo-Saxon England 1959

Bone, Gavin
Anglo-Saxon Poetry 1943

Brown, G. Baldwin
The Arts in Early England

Cam, H. M.
Liberties and Communities in Mediaeval England

Cambridge Mediaeval History

Chadwick, H. M.
The Heroic Age
Studies in Early English History

Chaucer, Geoffrey
Canterbury Tales

Collingswood, W. G.
Scandinavian Britain

Darby, H. C., *ed.*
Historical Geography of England 1936

Dasent, G. W.
The Story of Burnt Njal

Du Chaillu, Paul B.
The Viking Age

Duckett, Eleanor Shipley
The Gateway to the Middle Ages 1961

Eddas
The Poetic Edda (Bellows, *trans.*)
The Prose Edda (Brodeur, *trans.*)
The Younger Edda (Anderson, *trans.*)

Furnivall, Frederick J., *ed.*
Caxton's Book of Curtesye

Gaimar, Maistre Geffrei
Lestorie des Engles v. 2
Hardy, Sir Thomas Duffus and
Martin, Charles Trice

Grattan, John Henry G., and Singer, Charles
Anglo-Saxon Magic and Medicine 1952

Hartley, Dorothy
Mediaeval Costume and Life

Hight, G. A.
The Saga of Grettir the Strong

Hodgkin, R. H.
History of the Anglo-Saxons

Hulme, Edward Maslin
The Middle Ages

Jessup, Ronald
Anglo-Saxon Jewelry

Kirby, W. F., *trans.*
The Kalevala

Kendrick, T. D.
A History of the Vikings
Late Saxon and Viking Art

Kennedy, Charles W. (Verse Trans.)
Beowulf: the Oldest English Epic 1940
Anthology of Old English Poetry 1960

La Croix, Paul
Manners, Customs and Dress during the Middle Ages

La Monte, John L.
The World of the Middle Ages

Langland, Robert or William
Visions from Piers Plowman (Nevell Coghill, *trans.*)

Lethridge, T. C.
Herdsmen and Hermits

Loomis, Laura A. (Hibbard)
Three Middle English Romances

Mallet, Paul H.
Northern Antiquities (Bishop Percy, *trans.*)

Mediaeval Academy of America, publ. No. 52
Loomis, C. G.
White Magic

Mitchell, Edward Blair
The Art and Practice of Hawking 1959

Nicol, W.
The Ancient English Romance of Havelok the Dane

Norris, Herbert
Costume and Fashion v. 1, Earlier Ages

Olrick, Axel
Viking Civilization

Osborn, Edward Bollard
The Middle Ages

Oxford Dictionary of English Christian Names Withycomb, *ed* 1945

Oxford Concise Dictionary of English Place Names Ekwall, *ed* 1960

Phillpotts, Bertha S.
The Elder Edda

Quennell, Marjorie and C. H. B.
Everyday Life in Roman and Anglo-Saxon Times 1959

Raine, Angelo
Mediaeval York

Salzmann, Louis Francis
English Life in the Middle Ages 1926
Mediaeval Byways

Sayles, G. O.
The Mediaeval Foundations of England

Shepherd, W. R.
Atlas of Mediaeval and Modern History
Historical Atlas 1956

Skandinavia Past and Present
From the Viking Age to Absolute Monarchy 1961

Skeat, Rev. Walter W., *ed.*
The Lay of Havelok the Dane

Snorri Sturluson
Heimskringla 1948

Stenton, F. M.
Anglo-Saxon England 1947
The Danes in England

Stephenson, Carl
Mediaeval History: Europe from the 2nd to the 16th Century 1951

Strayer, J. R., and Munro, D. C.
The Middle Ages, 395–1500 1959
Western Europe in the Middle Ages 1955

Thompson, James Westfall and Johnson, Edgar
Introduction to Mediaeval Europe 1937

Thompson, Alexander H.
Bede

Thorndyke, Lynn
History of Mediaeval Europe

Waddell, L. A., *trans.*
The British Edda

Woods, G. B., Watt, H. A., and Anderson, G. K.
The Literature of England 1941

E21